THE EMERALD

Cassandra Moon knows her mother Dora has a special talent — but will it be enough to protect the eccentric older lady when she is abducted in the depths of winter? Once again, Cass finds herself teaming up with DI Noel Raven, whom she argues with and is attracted to in equal measures. But the only way she and Noel can save Dora is to accept the bond of love that joins them together, so they can harness the power of the emerald ring and bring down the evil Constantine . . .

FAY CUNNINGHAM

THE EMERALD
The Moonstones Trilogy

Complete and Unabridged

LINFORD
Leicester

First published in Great Britain in 2015

First Linford Edition
published 2016

A catalogue record for this book is available
from the British Library.

ISBN 978–1–4448–2981–5

Published by
F. A. Thorpe (Publishing)
Anstey, Leicestershire

Set by Words & Graphics Ltd.
Anstey, Leicestershire
Printed and bound in Great Britain by
T. J. International Ltd., Padstow, Cornwall

This book is printed on acid-free paper

1

Cassandra Moon moved away from the kitchen window. There was nothing to see on the other side of the glass except the garden and the path leading down to the gate. Mid-February frosts had left the trees leafless, the few surviving plants hanging their heads in misery, a hungry bird pecking at their roots. The kitchen was warm, but the temperature outside was falling fast.

Not for the first time, Cass cursed the small, pretty woman who had brought her into the world. Her mother had promised to catch the three o'clock bus home. Now it was nearly half past four, already getting dark, and Dora wasn't answering her mobile phone. Cass remembered seeing her mother drop the phone in her bag as she went out of the door, so she definitely had it with her. If she'd missed the bus home, the least she could do was phone or text so Cass wouldn't be tying herself in knots with worry.

Between staring out of the window and checking the phone, Cass paced the kitchen floor. She was beginning to wonder if she ought to notify the police or start phoning the hospitals. She needed to do something more productive than pacing. But the fact that her fifty-five-year-old mother was a bit late getting home was hardly enough to warrant a search party or a heat-seeking helicopter.

Sighing with frustration, she picked up her phone and keyed in the number of the local police station. The whole thing was beginning to get annoying. 'Can I speak to Noel Raven, please?' She gave her name and was told to hold on. A few minutes later she heard a voice she recognised — but it wasn't Noel.

'I'm sorry, Cass,' Brenda Stubbs told her. 'He got called out about half an hour ago. Some domestic disturbance. Can I help?'

'I don't think so, Brenda. I'm probably just being silly, but my mother went out to visit a friend and she's late back. Nearly an hour late. I'm worried because it's starting to get dark, and it's the first time she's been anywhere on her own for quite a while.'

'She's probably just forgotten the time. Has she got her phone with her?'

'Yes, but she's not answering.'

'I'll get Noel to ring you when he gets back. Give your mum another half hour, and if she's not back by then ring us again.'

'Thanks, Brenda.'

Cass dropped the phone back in its holder. The next bus wasn't due for twenty minutes, and she couldn't wait around that long without doing anything. She absently rubbed the ring on her finger and then looked down, half-expecting a genie to pop out. She had seen stranger things happen in this house. But the star sapphire just pulsed gently like it always did. Sometimes the stone felt hot, sometimes cold, but it never failed to give her comfort. Once, not so long ago, it had saved her life.

Grabbing a warm fleece jacket from a hook on the door, Cass quickly scribbled a note for her mother, picked up her car keys, and let herself out of the house. It was bitterly cold, and that brought on more worries. Dora had been well wrapped up when she left, but Cass was now convinced something bad had happened to her mother. She scraped a thin layer of ice from the windscreen of her little car and climbed in, turning up the heating as far as it would go. Icy cold air blasted out of the vents before she could turn the fan off. The engine fired up reluctantly and she eased out onto the road.

Dora's friend lived on the other side of the village, but the drive only took fifteen minutes. She had been to Mary Shelton's house several times before, recently to drop off a bottle of herbal remedy her mother had prepared; but as she turned into the narrow lane her foot slammed on the brake.

A police car blocked the road in front of her, and another had pulled up on the grass verge. Parked right outside the house where Mary lived, Cass saw a car she knew belonged to Detective Inspector Noel Raven. This must have been where he had gone on his call-out to the domestic disturbance.

Fear had already formed a cold lump in her chest, but the sight of an ambulance in the drive turned the rest of her body to ice. It never occurred to her for one minute that all the activity might have nothing to do with her mother. She knew it did. As she climbed out of her car, two men pushed a wheeled stretcher out through the front door of the house. On the stretcher was a body almost completely covered by a hospital blanket.

Cass started towards the house at a run but a tall man moved forward and stopped her, grabbing her arm. She struggled for a moment before she realised who had hold of her. The detective was big enough to block her progress without a great deal of effort.

'Noel?' She didn't want to waste time talking to him. The stretcher was already being loaded into the ambulance. 'I don't know what happened here, Noel, but I have to go to my mother. Please don't stop me.'

'Your mother?' The detective eased his grip on Cass's arm, a frown on his face. 'What has Pandora got to do with this?'

Cass's heart rate began to slow down. 'That isn't my mother on the stretcher?'

'No, it definitely isn't your mother. Right this minute I don't know who it is, but I would imagine it's the woman who lives in the house, a Mrs Mary Shelton. She fell down the stairs and hit her head. She's being taken to the hospital because she's still unconscious. What are you doing here, Cass? Do you know the woman?'

'Not really.' Cass could feel a headache coming on, the pain briefly pushing the worry to one side. 'But my mother knows her. Dora came here this afternoon to visit Mary.' She looked around vaguely, trying to focus. 'Is my mother still in the house?'

'There's no one in the house apart from a couple of police officers. Come and sit in my car and tell me what this is all about.'

Cass shook her head and winced as pain sliced behind her eyes, blurring her vision. 'My mother hasn't come home, so she must be in there. Perhaps she's hurt as well. Have you searched the house?' She tried to pull away, but Noel held on to her.

'No one else is in that house, Cass. Believe me, it's been thoroughly searched. Your mother is probably home by now. Why don't you try ringing her?'

Cass pulled her phone out of her bag, looking for any messages. 'I left her a note telling her to phone me if she got back first. There are no missed calls or messages.'

'Phone her anyway. I'll get someone to check the adjoining houses in case your mother went to get help for Mrs Shelton. Come and sit in the car out of the cold. We can't go inside the house for the moment because the forensic team is in there.'

'Why?'

'Because we might contaminate the scene.'

'I mean, why is a forensic team in there?' She could feel the panic coming back, bringing with it the strange dancing hieroglyphics of a migraine. 'What happened in that house, Noel?'

He opened the passenger door to his car. 'Sit in there for a minute, Cass. I'll check with the officers in the house and find out if they know anything about your mother.' He turned on the engine and switched the heat up to full. 'Don't move until I get back.'

Usually, being told what to do by Noel Raven annoyed Cass, but right now she was glad to have someone else take over. He might be a bit of a pain sometimes, but his tall, solid presence was reassuring. She called home without any real hope of a reply. Something bad had happened in the house where Mary Shelton lived, and her mother was part of it.

She listened to the answer phone pick up. She didn't leave a message; instead she fished in her bag until she found a packet of painkillers, and popped a couple in her mouth. A few moments later Noel Raven opened the car door and slid in beside her. A whiff of citrus aftershave followed him, and even in her present anxious state she felt the usual spark of electricity.

'They found a handbag under a chair which might be your mother's. It's got a phone still inside it.' He held up a green canvas tote embroidered with flowers. Is this your mother's?'

She nodded mutely. She wouldn't cry in front of Noel.

'Look inside and check the contents for me, Cass. Later on we'll need an inventory of everything, but right now I just want you to look inside and tell me what you see. Tell me if anything looks out of place. First impressions, OK?' She nodded again and took a deep breath. She had a rough idea of what her mother carried in her handbag, but it still felt like an invasion of her privacy.

There wasn't much in the bag, so it didn't take long. Noel asked her to open her mother's coin purse and check that as well. Dora hadn't been carrying a lot of money; enough change for her bus fare home, a couple of five-pound notes, and a debit card. There was a handbag-sized pack of tissues, lipstick, a perfume atomiser, and a small bag of herbs with a drawstring top. Cass pushed everything to one side, holding up the little bag of herbs so Noel could see it. 'She carries this for protection, but it obviously didn't work.' At the bottom of the bag she found seven or eight business cards and her mother's phone — plus a folded tissue. She was about to push the tissue aside with everything else, but then she paused. She could feel something small and hard inside the soft paper. 'There's something inside the tissue. Is this what you meant by anything unusual?'

'That depends on what it is.' Noel watched as Cass unfolded the tissue, then his eyes widened. 'Yeah, I guess that's what I meant.'

Cass held a gold ring in the palm of her hand — a thick gold band with a large green stone in the centre. 'It's pretty, isn't it? Heavy, too. Not meant for a woman.'

'Real?'

She hefted the ring again and then bent her head to look at it more closely. 'It looks like gold, but there's no hallmark that I can see. It might have been made abroad somewhere. The stone is definitely an emerald, square-cut and a good colour, but it has flecks in it, impurities of some sort.' She lifted her head. 'I would say it was definitely made for a man rather than a woman, and I've never seen it before, so I have no idea why my mother had it in her bag.'

Noel didn't answer for a minute. 'Is it valuable?'

'It depends what the setting is made of, and the impurities in the stone would detract from the value. A few hundred pounds at a rough guess.' She held the ring up to the light from the car window. 'The design is really unusual. Quite old, I would think.' She saw the expression on the detective's face. 'What's up?'

'Things have just got a bit more complicated, that's all. We need to find your mother.'

'I've been telling you that for the last half hour. If she's not at home and she's not in Mary's house, then something has happened to her.'

'Mary Shelton fell all the way down to the bottom of the stairs and hit her head on her mother's stair-lift. I've now been told there is a distinct possibility Mrs Shelton's fall wasn't an accident.

Someone had been in the house looking for something. Both the bedrooms are a mess. Drawers pulled out, things on the floor, a jewellery box emptied.'

'Mrs Shelton's mother is dead,' Cass told him. 'Mary's mother died a couple of weeks ago. We went to the funeral. That's partly why Dora was visiting her today, to make sure she's managing OK on her own. That's about all I can tell you.'

'Why would your mother have that ring in her bag?'

Cass turned round in her seat, a frown on her face. 'Are you suggesting my mother pushed Mary down the stairs and stole the ring from her? Where do you think Dora's gone now then? Jumped on a boat to the Bahamas?'

Noel sighed. 'Don't be ridiculous, Cass. I'm just saying it's got more complicated. If someone was searching for something specific, it could very well have been that ring. I'll put out a search request for Dora and hope she's found really soon. It's getting colder by the minute. I need to stay here for a bit but I can get someone to take you home.'

'Now you're the one being ridiculous. I've got a car, and I'm perfectly capable of driving.' It suddenly hit her like a blow to the chest. Her mother was lost out there somewhere in the cold and dark. She clutched Noel's arm. 'Where is she, Noel? Why are these special powers I'm supposed to have never around when I need them?'

He reached across and put his hand on her knee. 'We may be able to cook up a storm between us, but I can't see that helping your mother. Besides, she can manage a bit of magic herself when she needs to. She's a tough little lady.' He got out of the car and came round to open Cass's door. 'Do you have a photo of your mother? I can send someone round to pick it up and it'll help if we go door to door.'

She reached into her bag and pulled out a leather wallet. She always carried a photo of her mother. Up until a few months ago, Dora was the only family she had. The photo wasn't very recent — Cass had snapped her mother in the garden when she wasn't looking — but it was the best she could do.

Noel glanced at the picture and pushed it into his pocket. 'What was she wearing?'

'A cream duffle coat with a mauve pashmina. And she was wearing a mauve woollen hat, like a beret, as well. Oh, and gloves.' Cass had made sure her mother was well wrapped up before she left the house, but she knew that wouldn't help if Dora was out in the cold for long.

'Do you know how to contact your father? He needs to know his wife is missing, and he might have some idea where to find her.'

Cass hadn't seen her father since before Christmas. 'I have no idea where he is, but my mother must have some way of contacting him. I'll look for a telephone number when I get home.' As she got out of the car, Noel held out his arms and she went into them, feeling the fizz of electricity that always bound them together. The warmth from his body enfolded her. 'I need you, Noel.'

'I know you do.' He kissed her lightly on the forehead. 'I'll come over as soon as I'm finished here. About another hour. Go straight home and get in touch with your father. He can help us in a way no one else can.'

Cass ignored Noel's advice and drove around the lanes for half an hour, hoping to see her mother. Ice was beginning to form on the grass verges. She didn't think Dora could survive a night out in the open.

Cass hadn't seen much of Noel recently. He had spent Christmas with his mother and sister in Kent, and then come back to deal with the New Year's Eve crowd piling out of Norton's night clubs. Dora had cooked Christmas dinner for Cass and her friend, Liz, and Cass and her mother had spent New Year's Eve watching a movie. It had been a quiet but pleasant holiday, uneventful up until now.

Cass drove home slowly, knowing her mother wouldn't be there. She could feel the emptiness of the house before she turned into the drive. Tobias, their big golden tomcat, was waiting for her. She bent down to stroke a hand along his back, watching his black stripes ripple in the wake of her fingers. Tobias looked more like a small tiger than a domestic cat, a hint of something feral glinting in his amber eyes.

'Where is she, Tobias? Do you know where is she?' When he didn't respond, she smiled, and went looking for her mother's address book.

Fifteen minutes later, after going through each page searching for some clue to her father's contact address or telephone number, she gave up and put the kettle on. Hector worked for some obscure government office and changed his identity on a regular basis. Everything about his job was very hush-hush, so perhaps Dora had never written anything down.

Cass poured herself a cup of tea and sat at the kitchen table. She supposed she could go to her studio and do some work with her jewellery, but her head was a mess and she knew she wouldn't be able to concentrate. All she could do was wait for Noel to come back and hope he had some news. She took a sip of her tea, and then spotted her mother's iPad on the arm of the sofa. That was a much more likely place to store Hector's telephone number. By the time she had opened every file she could think of and studied every list of contacts, her tea was stone cold. She got up to put the mug in the microwave and suddenly remembered seeing a name on the address list that didn't make sense: Tobias H. Moon. She must have said the name out loud, because her mother's big cat jumped up on the table and stood looking at her.

'You don't really need an email address, do you, cat?' She went back to her mother's tablet and scrolled down the list until she found the name again. The only means of contacting Tobias H. Moon was by mobile phone. She tapped in the numbers and breathed a sigh of relief when she heard a dial tone. Her father answered almost immediately.

'Cassandra?'

'Something has happened to Dora,' she told him, her voice catching. 'She's gone missing.'

He was silent for a couple of seconds. 'Give me five minutes and I'll call you back.'

He was probably in a room full of people, she thought, and needed to go somewhere quiet to talk to her, but waiting five minutes was difficult. Hector always sounded completely in control, as if he didn't care. But she knew he did.

He called back after four minutes. She knew because she had been staring at her watch. 'I'm on my way right now, Cassandra. I'll be there by morning. Listen to me — I know you're worried about your mother, but she will be fine. She's somewhere warm and she's not hurt. I'd know if she was. I'll see you tomorrow.'

'How do you — ' Cass began, but he had already disconnected.

2

Dora knew better than to argue with a man holding a knife. As soon as the knife was waved in her face, she decided to go quietly. Well, almost.

'You have to call an ambulance,' she told him.

The man who had been holding the knife against her throat didn't answer. His face was grim, but she took her time getting into the car, weighing up her options. The houses in the lane were well spaced out, but not isolated. There was a light in the window of the house next door, but Dora knew she wouldn't make it out of Mary's driveway before the man caught up with her. Then what? She'd be back where she started, and he'd be even more watchful. She let him strap her into the passenger seat and walk round to the driver's side. If she didn't do anything to upset him, he might drop his guard a little. She was in her mid-fifties, not much over five feet tall, and quite good at doing the frightened little woman act.

'You really ought to call an ambulance,' she told him again, the quiver in her voice not all pretence.

He started the engine and took off in a shower of gravel, shooting out onto the main road without looking either way. 'What's the point? You saw her. She's dead. They'll see her room was trashed and think I pushed her deliberately. I'm not going to prison for murdering an old lady. Not when it wasn't my fault.'

Dora decided to try a different approach. 'You can't be sure she's dead. She hit her head at the bottom of the stairs. She may just have knocked herself out. Please call someone. If there's any chance at all that she's still alive, you have to call an ambulance. If she's still alive and you leave her to die, you will be a murderer.'

He was quiet for a minute, obviously thinking things through. She took that as a good sign. She was cold and frightened, but she was more worried about her friend, Mary. The woman had been still and silent at the bottom of the stairs, and there had been blood on the carpet beneath her head. That didn't necessarily mean she was dead, but it did mean she needed help quickly. Dora had tried to get close to see if she could do anything to help, but the big man had stopped her. He had looked at the woman's still body and seen all the blood, and panic had taken over. That was when he had dashed into the kitchen and pulled a knife from the rack.

'You phone, then, if you're that worried. I can't call anyone while I'm driving, can I? It would be just my luck to get stopped by the police.'

'I don't have a phone,' Dora said patiently. 'My phone is in my bag, and you wouldn't let me bring my bag with me.'

He fumbled with his seatbelt, trying to get a hand in his pocket, swearing profusely all the time. Eventually he pulled out a phone and thrust it at her. 'Just call an ambulance and give them the address of the house. Nothing else or I'll cut your bloody hands off.'

Dora thought he would have a hard job cutting off her hands and driving at the same time, but she wasn't going to put it to the test. His mood was volatile enough already. She tapped in the numbers and gave the information he told her to. Before she could say any more, he ripped the phone out of her hands. If he'd let her keep hold of the phone for another second, she could have told the operator who she was and that might have stopped Cassie worrying about her, but she had done the best she could in the circumstances.

'Where are you taking me?'

'I'm not answering questions, so shut up.'

Dora tried to decide what to do next. She hadn't used any proper spells for some time, and experimenting in a fast-moving car wasn't a good idea; she might turn him into a frog by mistake. She would have to wait and see what other opportunities presented themselves. The man seemed to have a plan of some sort — he wasn't just driving about aimlessly — but it would make her feel much better if she had some idea of their destination.

The old car he was driving was struggling to pump out any heat, and Dora was beginning to feel chilled. With a quick glance at her captor, she closed her eyes and pushed the temperature in the car up a few degrees. Just enough to keep her comfortable. She smiled to herself. She might be out of practice, but she could still conjure up a bit of warmth when she needed it.

She was surprised when they pulled onto a snow-covered farm track with nothing in sight but a couple of farm cottages. It was almost dark now, and there were no lights in the windows of the cottages, but the gleam of the snow made everything stand out in sharp relief. Unending white fields stretched away as far as Dora could see. There were a few trees visible behind the houses, but otherwise they might just as well have been on the moon. Making a run for it in this weather was out of the question.

Her captor got out of the car first, taking the car keys with him. Dora watched him open the front door to one of the houses and go inside. She felt frustrated. She was a witch with magic powers and could probably have started the car engine, but she had never learned to drive; and even if she could figure out the mechanics, she didn't know how long it would take her to reach civilisation. Getting stuck in a snow drift would put her in a worse situation than the one she was in already.

Before she could make up her mind what to do, he was back, shouting at her to get out of the car. Once she was standing in the snow, he grabbed her arm and dragged her up the icy path to the house.

'Whose house is it?' she asked, struggling to keep her feet. He pulled her inside and closed the door behind them. As she had expected, the house was dark and freezing cold.

'None of your business. Just in case you're wondering, the house next door is empty as well. This house belonged to someone's mother. Now she's gone.'

The front door opened directly into a small living room, and Dora could see what looked like a kitchen through another door. A staircase took up most of one wall, leaving just enough room for an old beige sofa and chair. There was also a small table with two wooden chairs pushed tightly underneath. The bare boards on the living room floor had a pale rectangle where a rug had been.

The man walked into the kitchen and clicked the light switch. When nothing happened he tried a switch on the wall. 'The power is off,' he said as he opened a cupboard and reached inside. 'The gas was turned off at the mains as well, but I've turned it on again.'

'Don't turn the gas ring on,' Dora warned as he reached for a knob on the cooker. 'It won't light by itself without electricity; you need a match.'

'I haven't got a match, or a lighter. And I don't smoke, so don't ask.' He was getting twitchy now, anger beginning to surface. He slammed the oven door shut. 'The power is always going off in these places. I bet the old girl had some candles somewhere.'

'If there are candles, there must be matches. We just have to find them. I'll help you look.'

Dora found the candles in one of the kitchen cupboards. The matches were in a drawer above. Both the oven and the hob were run by gas, so she lit all the rings, and the kitchen was soon warm. She guessed the cottages used bottled gas, so it wouldn't last forever, but she wasn't going to think about that. A flowered canister that had been left behind on a shelf held a few teabags, and there was another tin half-full of old digestive biscuits. It didn't take Dora long to boil a small pan of water and have a pot of tea on the table, together with a saucer of biscuits. She put a knitted tea-cosy on the pot and found china cups and saucers in another cupboard. There was no milk, but Dora took her tea without milk anyway, and her captor seemed glad of the warm liquid.

'This lady had some pretty china,' she said.

'Yes.' He picked up the cup as if it might break. 'And it looks like she had to leave it all here, in her old house. That's probably what killed her. Old people don't like being moved.'

'You knew her, then, did you?'

'No, I didn't know her. Stop asking stupid questions.'

Dora sighed. 'What are you going to do?' she asked. 'People will be looking for both of us. I don't think you killed Mrs Shelton, but if we go back into town you can find out for sure.'

'What if I did kill her? They put me inside once for punching a policeman. The police already think I'm violent. If I go inside for killing that old lady, I'll never get out.'

'What were you looking for at the house? I was in the other room when you arrived, but I heard you shouting and banging about. What were you looking for upstairs?'

'I was looking for a ring. An emerald set in gold brought back here from abroad. Someone wants it, and I know it's in the house somewhere. I asked her nicely, but she wouldn't tell me where it was.'

'So you pushed her down the stairs?'

'No! I told you I didn't push her.' He was shouting now. 'She fell. The silly old bat just fell.'

'What did you want the ring for? Were you going to sell it?'

He put his teacup down and shook his head. 'Not sell it. I told you, someone wanted it. I owe money. If I get the ring, I'm off the hook. Simple as that.'

'That doesn't give you the right to steal it.'

Mary Shelton had given Dora the ring to show Cassandra, and maybe get an estimate of its value. Dora had put the ring in her handbag, but when she heard someone shouting and crashing about upstairs she kicked her bag under a chair. She heard Mary cry out, and then the thump as she fell, but by the time Dora rushed into the hall her friend was already unconscious at the foot of the staircase.

'The old girl doesn't need it. It's probably been lying around in that house for years.' He prowled the room. 'I've got to pay back the money I owe or he'll kill me. I know he will.'

'Who's going to kill you? Maybe if you tell the police — '

He stopped her with a dry laugh. 'You don't know what you're talking about, lady. Why don't you shut up and stop asking questions. If you'd minded your own business in the first place, just stayed where you were instead of rushing out to get a look at me, you wouldn't be here now.' He warmed his hands in front of the oven. 'I'm hungry. Did you find anything else to eat?'

Dora shook her head. 'Only those biscuits, and they were past their sell-by date.'

He started pacing again. 'I need to find out what to do with you. He told me not to call him on the phone, not ever, but I need to know what to do with you.' He looked at his watch, his hands clenching and unclenching nervously. 'I need to see him tonight so I can find a way out of this mess.'

'Who is this man? Who are you afraid of?'

He shouted at her then, and she backed away. He had got himself into a situation he couldn't handle, and she knew that pushing him any further would be a big mistake. His next few sentences were laced with expletives, some she had heard before and some she hadn't, but he finished up telling her he was going to lock her in one of the bedrooms.

'I'll freeze to death,' she said. 'I'm not going to try to escape on foot, am I? Not while it's still snowing. You don't have to lock me in.'

He laughed at her. 'Please yourself. If I were you I'd make a run for it. It'd solve all my problems if you died out there in the snow. I'll even leave the door open for you.' He zipped his padded jacket up as high as it would go and pulled a pair of gloves out of his pocket. 'If you're not here when I get back, I'm not coming looking for you, so mind you don't get lost.' He laughed again, and then walked out into the still-falling snow, leaving the front door wide open.

Dora shut the door and pushed the temperature in the room up a few degrees. If the man drove into a ditch, then no one would know where she was. But at least he wasn't going to kill her and bury her body in the snow. She couldn't quite make him out. He hadn't tried to hurt her, and he didn't seem a really bad person, but something had caused him to force his way into a house and try to rob an old lady.

She felt a small shiver of apprehension when she heard him drive away, but now that she was alone she could work out how to get a message to Cassie — and then plan her own escape.

*   *   *

Cass knew Noel would come over as soon as he could, but the old house she had lived in all her life seemed cold and silent, almost scary, without the warm presence of her mother.

She had thought about living on her own, but in the last six months Dora had been unable to leave the house. The doctors called it traumatic agoraphobia; her mother just called it a spell. Cass knew she had made her mother's illness an excuse not to look for a place of her own — she knew Dora was perfectly cable of looking after herself — but the arrangement seemed to work. The house was big enough for both of them to have their own space. The garage had been converted into a studio for Cass's jewellery business, registered as Moonstones, and Dora had an office on the ground floor where she sold her herbal remedies online.

By the time Noel arrived through the back door in a flurry of cold air and wet snow, Cass had taken to pacing the floor again. 'It's a bitch of a night out there,' he said, and then looked at Cass apologetically. 'We're doing everything we can to find your mother. I'm as worried about her as you are.'

'I know you are, and thank you for that. Tea or alcohol?' she asked him.

'I've finished for tonight, and I was thinking I might stay here. You probably need the company, and if I stay the night I can have a drink. I feel I need one.'

She felt a huge surge of relief when

he suggested staying, and then mentally berated herself for being such a wimp. She was a grown woman; she ought to be able to manage a night in the house without her mother.

'Thank you. I'd like you to stay, but you'll have to sleep in the guest bedroom.'

He grinned at her. 'Of course. Where else would I sleep?'

'I managed to contact my father,' she told him, ignoring his comment. 'Hector said he'll be here tomorrow morning. Early, by the sound of it. He also said Dora is OK. He said she's not hurt. He'd know if she was.'

Noel nodded agreement. 'Yes, he would. The same way I'd know if anything bad happened to you. Does he know where she is?'

Cass shook her head. 'His talents obviously don't stretch that far.'

She found a bottle of whisky in a cupboard and poured Noel a double shot. She filled her own glass with a deep red Shiraz. 'There's a pot of lamb stew that just needs heating up, and I know my mother made bread yesterday. Have a look in the fridge.'

Noel found the bread, and a bundle of green leaves. 'Is this salad?'

'Whatever it is, it must be edible. Dora never puts any of her concoctions in the fridge, only stuff that can be eaten. I think she calls that a field salad. Leaves from the banks and hedgerows. They usually taste all right. When she was stuck in the house because of her agoraphobia, she'd get a team of schoolboys to fill a bag with green stuff, and then she'd sort through it and pay them for anything edible.'

Noel looked at the bundle suspiciously. 'Do I need to wash it?'

'Not if it was in the fridge. Just throw it in a bowl, it'll be fine.'

The meal was delicious, even if it was slightly unusual. The stew was hot and spicy, the bread warm and crusty, and the salad crisp and peppery. Noel switched from whisky to wine and topped up Cass's glass. For a moment she wondered if he was trying to get her drunk, but he looked about ready to fall asleep, so she doubted he had an ulterior motive.

She was just starting to clear the table when something tapped on the window. For a moment they both stared at the heavy drapes covering the glass.

'What was that?' Cass asked, glad Noel was standing beside her.

He reached for the curtain to draw it back, but then the sound came again: a sudden spurt of little taps, like gravel hitting the glass from the outside. Holding up his hand to silence her, he moved to the side of the window and grabbed the curtain with one hand, pulling it back. Cass peered nervously at the window, but she couldn't see anything except darkness. No ghostly face peering at her through the glass, no disembodied hand about to tap on the window again.

Noel turned round and put a finger to his lips. 'Keep quiet for a minute,' he told her. 'I'm going to open the window.'

Cass didn't think that was a good idea, but before she could say anything he pushed up the sash window and a pigeon hopped inside. The bird stood on the windowsill trembling, its feathers fluffed up with fear. Noel gently picked it up and stroked it until it settled. 'It's scared silly, but it still came inside.'

'Is it hurt, do you think?' Cass asked. 'Or just cold?' Cass moved slowly toward the table, expecting the bird to back away. Instead, it put its head on one side and looked at her with one eye, as if it wasn't quite sure what species she belonged to. She felt as if she had been judged — and failed miserably.

'It's not a pigeon, is it?' she said to Noel. 'It's a collared dove.'

'Still in the pigeon family, but smaller and prettier than a wood pigeon.' He bent down and peered at the bird. 'I don't think it's hurt . . . ' The bird made a cooing sound similar to a purr, and Noel smiled. 'I think Dora sent it.'

Cass rolled her eyes. 'The bird is talking to you now, is it?'

'No, of course not.' She thought he looked slightly embarrassed. 'Just a feeling I have, that's all. She sent me a bird once before, if you remember.'

'Yes, I remember it well. You accidentally hit the bird with your car and killed it, so she's not likely to do the same thing again.'

The collared dove settled down on the table and closed its eyes. For a moment Cass thought it might be dead, but she could see it was still trembling. Noel ran a hand down the bird's back, smoothing its feathers. 'It doesn't want to be here, you can see how scared it is, but something is making it stay.' He turned his hand over and looked at his palm with a frown. 'Ink or paint,' he said. 'There's something on the bird's back. I've got ink on my hand.' He peered at the feathers he'd just touched. 'It looks as if someone tried to draw something on the bird's feathers.

Something like a holly leaf.'

Before Cass could take a closer look the bird got to its feet and flapped its wings, fluffing its feathers up again. Down on the floor Tobias made an interested little noise at the back of his throat. Not quite a growl, but pretty close. The pigeon moved nervously to the middle of the table.

'Back off, Toby,' Noel told the cat. 'If you think he's a home delivery meal, you're wrong.'

Cass picked the big cat up in her arms and put him out in the hall, much to the cat's obvious disgust, but she knew Tobias could kill the bird with one paw tied behind his back. With the cat out of the room the bird settled down again, and Cass was able to have a good look at the feathers on its back. Close to, there appeared to be a few random black marks on the feathers, but when she stood back a little she could see an outline of something, something with spiky bits, possibly a holly leaf, but it could be practically anything. Noel had smudged the drawing to a point where it was unrecognisable.

'The bird probably flew against some wet paint,' she said. She saw the expression on Noel's face and held her hands in the air. 'What? You can't really expect me to believe my mother drew a picture on a pigeon and then sent the bird here.' She knew it was exactly the sort of thing her mother would do, but she wasn't going to admit that to Noel. 'Anyway, what's the picture of a holly leaf supposed to tell us?'

'Possibly where she's being held. Something she can see out of a window, maybe, like a holly bush. And if you're prepared to believe it might be from her, it also tells us she's still alive. She must know you're worrying about her. She'd want you to know she's safe. It also means she's not too far away. The bird would have been exhausted if it had flown far in this weather.'

Cass bent down to peer at the pigeon. 'It looks a bit tired now.'

Noel sighed with frustration. 'I

shouldn't have touched it. I should know better than to mess with a clue, and it's the only one we've got at the moment.' The bird stood up and Noel tipped the breadcrumbs from his plate on to the table. 'It might want something to eat before it leaves.'

Cass watched the bird daintily peck at the crumbs. 'It's a good job you have an affinity with birds. I'd have set the cat on it.'

'No, you wouldn't.'

'No, of course I wouldn't. But I don't understand birds like you do. I have my stones instead.' Tobias scratched on the door and Cass opened it to let him in. 'Behave yourself,' she told him sternly.

The bird finished the crumbs and stretched, making its feathers tremble, then it flew back to the windowsill, obviously ready to be let out. 'Are you sure you want to go out in this weather?' Noel asked, but when the bird didn't answer he opened the window and let it out into the night.

3

Cass made coffee and filled a little jug with cream. She tried really hard to accept all this magic business, and after all that had happened it shouldn't be difficult. When she thought about it, a messenger pigeon was almost normal. A collared dove with a picture on its back, not so normal, but her mother was a witch and her father a warlock, so 'normal' was not a word she used very often.

'I spent an hour in the office after I left the scene of the accident,' Noel said. 'I was trying to find out if Mary Shelton had any immediate family. It seems she has a son she doesn't see very often. A bit of a loser, according to the next-door neighbour. We're still trying to contact him. Her husband died when the son was ten years old, and he's a bit over twenty now. It must be difficult bringing up a child on your own, particularly a boy. When Mary's mother moved in with her a couple of years ago the son came round more often, so the neighbour says. Got on well with his grandma. But then she died, and Mrs Shelton was on her own again.' He added cream to his coffee and two spoons of sugar. 'Did your mother tell you anything that might help us find any relatives? We don't even know if the woman had any siblings.'

'I don't know if my mother knew Mary *had* a son. They weren't close friends. She knew Mary through her online herbal business. She went to see her because Mary's mother had died recently.'

Noel finished his coffee, took off his shoes, and stretched out his feet towards the heat of the big range. 'The problem is, we're working on two different cases at the same time. The ransacked bedroom points towards a crime rather than an accident, but there's no real connection between that and your mother's disappearance. I can only assume she saw something that frightened her enough to make her take off without her money or phone, or someone abducted her at the scene.' He looked at Cass. 'Can your mother defend herself? I know she can warm a room or make a light come on in the dark, but does she have any stronger aibilities?'

Cass shook her head miserably. 'I don't know. I really don't know. She's probably tried to tell me several times. I'm sure she wanted to tell me what she could do, but I didn't want to listen to her. I had my hands over my ears all the time because I was afraid of what I might hear. I was scared I might be like her, and I just wanted to be normal. My father left us when I was just a little girl, and she brought me up on her own.' Cass shook her head again. 'I still don't really know why he left.'

'Have you had time to check out the emerald ring? You identified your mother's bag, so until we can prove otherwise, the ring belongs to your mother. If I find out it has anything to do with the case, I may have to take it away as evidence, so it might be a good idea to find out as much as we can while we still have it.'

'I'd forgotten all about it.' Cass picked up her mother's bag and took out the tissue-wrapped ring. She held it on the palm of her hand for a minute and then closed her fingers round it. 'It's not telling me anything. It's just a nice emerald ring. Nothing special.' She handed it to him. 'Like I said, it's a man's ring.' Noel took the ring and she watched him slip it on his finger. 'It looks good on you.' It looked brighter, the green stone positively luminous. She thought she could see a gleam in the centre of the emerald that hadn't been there before.

Noel lifted his hand, holding the ring as far away from his body as he could. 'It feels strange.'

'How do you mean, strange?'

'Sort of bedded down into my finger.' He pulled at the ring. 'I don't think I can get it off.'

Cass gave him a look of disbelief. 'Are you kidding? It didn't look tight when you put it on.'

'I know that, but it's tight now.'

She took his hand and tried to turn the ring. It didn't budge, not even a fraction. 'We can try cooking oil, that might work. Otherwise it seems you're stuck with it, which might be a bit difficult to explain if it's needed as evidence.' She opened a cupboard, looking for a bottle of oil. 'Did you tell anyone that I had it?'

'No, but I can't exactly keep it hidden, can I? It sort of stands out.'

'Like a sore thumb.' Cass stifled a bubble of laughter. 'Sorry, I know it's not funny. Can I ask why you put it on your wedding finger?'

'I didn't, did I?' He looked down at his hand in surprise. 'I didn't know I had a special wedding finger. A man can wear a ring on any finger, can't he?'

'If you say so.' Cass watched him trying to prise the ring from his finger. 'You'll make your finger sore if you keep doing that.' She half-filled a glass tumbler with oil. 'Hold your finger in that for a few minutes.' She found the whole thing a bit puzzling. Gemstones often reacted strangely around her, but Noel had never had a problem before. 'There must be something different about that ring, or that particular gemstone. Is an emerald special to you in any way?'

He wriggled his finger about in the oil. 'I think it's my birthstone, but my birthday isn't until May.'

She handed him a cloth. 'It *is* your birthstone, then. Try easing the ring off with the cloth, twisting it rather than just pulling.'

He let out an audible sigh of relief when the ring slid off his finger. 'Thank goodness for that. I thought for a minute the only way to explain it to everyone was to marry you. You put me off last time, but I thought you might have changed your mind.'

She hadn't said no; she had just procrastinated a little, and when he hadn't pushed her for an answer she decided it was the champagne talking. Then he had barely spoken to her for more than three months. 'There you go, then,' she said. 'I'm glad I helped you out of that nasty predicament.' She held her hand out for the ring. 'I think I'd better hang on to that, don't you?'

'I'll take it to work tomorrow and lock it up in the police safe. If the trouble at Mary Shelton's house was about the ring, I don't want you to keep it here. We had the same sort of argument before Christmas about a certain sapphire, if you remember. This time I'm going to insist.'

Cass shrugged. 'OK. But for goodness sake, don't try it on again. Just lock it up until we know who really owns it.'

'Perhaps Mrs Shelton will sell it to me.' His forehead creased in a puzzled frown. 'It felt right on me for some reason, as if it belonged.'

'It would do if it's your birthstone, but don't get too attached to it; it's not yours.'

He yawned. 'I need to get some sleep, Cass.' He looked at his watch. 'So do you. It's pushing midnight. Show me where my bedroom is before I fall asleep standing up.'

'Can you phone the police station first and find out if there's any news about my mother?' For a little while Cass had forgotten her mother was missing, and that made her feel guilty. Her mother could be lying dead somewhere, and she was trading small talk with Noel.

'I told them to contact me at any time, day or night,' he said, 'and I have a lot of officers out looking for her and asking questions. If she was injured, or just wandering around lost, they would have found her by now. Whoever took her has tucked her away somewhere warm for the night. You have to believe Hector. Like he said, he'd know if she's been harmed in any way.'

'I wish he was here.' Cass took a breath. 'I did without him for so many years, but now he's not here, I miss him. Not that you haven't been great, Noel,' she added hastily. 'It's just that he radiates an aura of power. I don't know if it's something magical, or just that hint of danger my mother was talking about, but he makes me feel protected.'

'And I don't?' He sounded quite put out, and she smiled.

'No, you make me feel safe. There's a difference. You don't scare me like he does.'

'If I wasn't so tired, I'd make you take back those words. I can be really scary when I try. But for tonight we'll have to rely on Tobias to protect us both.'

When she paused outside his door, he put both hands on her shoulders and turned her towards him. 'Can I kiss you goodnight, Cass?'

'Are we going to start a tropical

storm, or set the house on fire?'

He shook his head. 'I promise you this will be a very tired, brotherly kiss.'

If she was truthful, she had been hoping for more, but a girl had to be thankful for small mercies. As it was, tiredness didn't come into the equation, and if she had a brother who kissed her like that she would have him locked up. A small thunderclap left a smell of ozone behind, and Tobias looked at them both reproachfully when his fur stood on end.

Noel eased her away and held her at arm's length. 'Perhaps I shouldn't have left it so long. I think I need to kiss you on a regular basis as a sort of desensitising process.'

'Then don't leave it for months without calling me.' She had meant the words to sound flippant, but they came out as a rather pathetic reproach.

Noel put his hand on the doorjamb to support himself. 'I can't think straight when I'm with you. I'm a policeman, Cass. I don't belong in your world. My mother isn't a witch.'

'Can you be sure of that?' Cass asked quietly. 'Both your parents were killed in a car crash when you were still a child. You don't know what they might have been.'

He looked at her without saying anything for a moment. 'What happens between us scares me, Cass, and I don't scare easy.' He turned the handle on the door and pushed it open. 'Go to bed. We'll talk in the morning.'

After he closed his door, she picked up Tobias and smoothed his fur. 'You only have yourself to blame,' she told him. 'You shouldn't have been snooping.'

⋆   ⋆   ⋆

Cass awoke to the rich smell of brewing coffee. She sat up in bed and rubbed her eyes, disoriented for a moment. Her mother made tea in the morning. Besides, it was only just past six a.m.

A few seconds later she flopped back

down on the bed. Her mother was still out there somewhere. If she'd been found, Noel would have told her even if he had to wake her to do so. She waited for the sick feeling in the pit of her stomach to return, but it didn't. Somehow she knew her mother was safe. Perhaps it was the appearance of the bird, or just that she had relaxed enough to listen to her heart. Like Hector, she would know immediately if her mother were dead. Yesterday she had felt confused and unsafe, probably exactly the way her mother had been feeling at the time, but this morning she felt refreshed and relatively calm. Noel was in the kitchen making coffee, and her father would arrive at any moment. She wasn't alone. She had all the help she could wish for.

She had a quick shower and pulled on jeans and a sweater. Without her mother there to keep the house warm, she could feel the cold creeping through the old timbers. Socks inside her old, comfy slippers helped, but hot coffee would be even better.

Noel was in the kitchen, but he wasn't alone. Her father smiled at her from his seat by the stove, Tobias on his lap. She smiled back, amused at the sight of her tall, rugged, seafaring father with the big golden cat stretched across his knees. He was sitting in the cat's favourite chair, so she supposed it was only right to make him share. The stove had been banked up, so the kitchen was warm and cosy. Noel handed her a mug of hot coffee and she pulled up a seat next to her father.

'Sorry I overslept. When did you get in?' She was never quite sure how to address her father. He intimidated her, although she knew he tried very hard not to. With his height and his weather-beaten skin, his thick hair only lightly flecked with grey, he looked more like an ancient warrior than a secret agent. Sometimes she almost believed he really was a warlock.

'About an hour ago. Noel was already up and about. He made coffee, and now he's doing something with some eggs. If you make some toast, Cassandra, we can all have breakfast. I need to get out there and make some enquires of my own once we've eaten.'

She tried very hard not to bristle. He might be her father, but until recently she hadn't seen him for almost twenty-five years. He hadn't earned the right to tell her what to do. Noel tried to boss her about as well, and she was getting fed up with it. She had lived with her mother for a long time, and they had managed fine on their own. She didn't need a couple of men to tell her how to behave.

Noel left his cooking to put an arm round her shoulders. 'Good morning to you, too.'

She smiled sheepishly. 'I'm sorry. Good morning, and thank you for staying with me last night. Is there any more news?'

'Not a lot, except Mary Shelton's son seems to have disappeared. He doesn't actually live with his mother, although his records say he does. My team did what they could, but you can't go calling on people late at night without a pretty good reason. I'll get a house-to-house up and running today and keep trying to track down her son. Someone might have seen something.'

'They must have, surely.' Cass found some bread and dropped four slices in the toaster. 'If someone tried to make my mother go somewhere she didn't want to go, she'd put up a fight.' She frowned. 'I don't understand how she could be abducted in broad daylight and no one see anything.'

Noel watched her butter the hot toast and put it on plates. 'It was cold outside,' he said, 'and most of the people in those bungalows are getting on a bit. They were probably curled up in front of the fire watching TV, rather than looking out of the window.'

'Dora would have made a noise,' Cass said stubbornly. 'She wouldn't have gone quietly.'

'The tip of a six-inch kitchen knife

blade pressed against your jugular can keep you quiet.' Hector stood up and dropped the cat back on his chair. He looked at Noel. 'You could get someone to check the kitchen knives. Unless the perpetrator went to the house already armed, he might have grabbed whatever was handy to subdue the women.'

'So Dora might have been stabbed,' Cass said quietly.

Hector shrugged. 'I doubt it. She's not stupid enough to take on a man with a knife, and spells are tricky. Get it wrong, and you make the situation worse than it was in the first place. Going quietly is sometimes the best option.' He sat down at the table and waited for Cass to put a plate in front of him. She had given him two slices of toast, and Noel heaped a pile of golden scrambled eggs on top. Hector picked up his knife and fork. 'It's a pity you couldn't get the bird to stay. I'd like to have seen Dora's drawing.'

Noel handed Cass a filled plate and sat down with his own breakfast. 'Some of the drawing was smudged, but what was left did look like a holly leaf.' He shook salt on his eggs, ignoring a disapproving look from Cass. 'But that doesn't help us much. There's quite a lot of holly about at this time of the year.'

'If it *was* from my mother, and she was trying to send us a message, why didn't she write something we could all understand?'

'A collared dove has dusty, sticky feathers,' Hector said. 'It's not like a nice white notepad. Besides, a rough drawing was probably all she had time for.' He looked at Cass curiously. 'Why don't you think your mother sent the message?'

She looked at him in disbelief. 'Who would draw a picture on a pigeon?'

'Your mother.' He turned to Noel. 'Can you draw it on a sheet of paper for me?'

With a sigh of resignation, Cass took a notepad from beside the telephone and picked up a pen. 'I'll do it. I went to art at school. I doubt a policeman has that on his CV.'

'You'd be surprised what I have on my CV.' Noel watched as she drew a rough outline on the pad. 'Yeah, that's what it looked like. There was something else, but I smudged whatever that was when I stroked the bird. All that was left was what Cass just drew. It does look like a holly leaf, doesn't it?'

Hector bent over the notepad, a frown on his face. 'There are other things it could be.'

'Like what?' Cass asked. She couldn't think of anything else that resembled her drawing.

'Like Noel said, whatever Pandora was trying to draw doesn't help us much at the moment. Straightforward police work is our best bet.'

She knew Hector was avoiding giving her a straight answer, but he lived a life of lies. She sometimes wondered if he ever told the whole truth. He had told her the reason he hadn't contacted her for over twenty years was because he wanted to keep her safe, but if that were true he had chosen a funny way of protecting her.

She cleared the table and loaded the washing machine while Noel and her father got ready to brave the cold. It had snowed overnight, a thin layer of white covering the path outside. She intended doing a bit of detective work of her own once the men had left, so she hoped her car would start.

* * *

Noel was already shrugging out of his jacket as he opened the door to his outer office. Brenda Stubbs and Kevin Green, two of his police detectives, were already at their computer screens. 'What have we got?' he asked them.

Kevin looked up. 'Morning, sir. Not a lot, actually. Nothing from the hospital or forensics to suggest it wasn't an accident — apart from the bedrooms being ransacked, of course.'

'How is Mrs Shelton? Can we interview her yet?' Noel ran a frustrated hand through his dark hair. 'She's the only one who knows what really happened.'

'I phoned the hospital half an hour ago,' Brenda told him. 'They've put Mrs Shelton in an induced coma to help her brain heal. Could be anything from a day to a week before they bring her round.'

Noel opened the connecting door to his own office. It was a small room made up mainly of partitioning, but with a large window and a view of the street below. He hadn't been in Norton long enough to make his mark on the small space, and he wasn't one for knickknacks, but he quite liked his little domain. He threw his jacket over the back of the visitor's chair and went back to the outer office.

'We need to set up an information board even if we haven't got much information,' he said. 'I take it there's no news on Pandora Moon?'

Brenda shook her head. 'I'm beginning to hope she *was* abducted. She wouldn't have survived last night if she's got herself lost or if she's fallen over somewhere.'

'I think she would have been found by now if that had happened. There was a pretty thorough search last night, and I left instructions for the search to continue at first light this morning. If she was on her own she couldn't have gone far; she didn't have time. Besides, she's not senile. She can't be much over fifty, and she's fully in command of her senses. She was going to get a bus home, so there was no reason for her to go walkabout in the dark.'

Kevin looked uncomfortable. 'She thinks she's a witch.'

The young detective seemed to think that explained everything. Did he think Pandora Moon was flying around Norton on a broomstick? Noel decided not to answer on the grounds that it might incriminate him. He was positive Dora was a witch. He just hoped she could cook up a spell to keep herself warm and safe. Outside his window, large white flakes had begun falling.

Kevin helped set up the whiteboard, and Noel wrote the names Mary Shelton and Dora Moon. Brenda had located the last known address for the son, but he wasn't living with his mother anymore. His name was Bradley, commonly known as Brad. He worked at a local call centre for an insurance company, and he had a record. There was a picture of him in a police line-up looking like a rabbit caught in the middle of a motorway; all big eyes and obvious fear. He didn't look particularly threatening. Noel waited while Brenda printed off the picture and then stuck it on the board.

'His offences are mainly debt-related court orders,' Brenda said. 'The line-up was for a burglary, but he wasn't picked out by the witness so he walked away free. He earns a pretty good salary, but he's maxed out on three credit cards and he has a bank overdraft in the red.'

'He's only got himself to look after, so what does he do with his money?'

'Gambles, by the look of it. Mostly online, but some local card games and roulette in the clubs and casinos. No betting shops anymore. He got himself a bit of a reputation, so the local ones won't let him through the door.'

'Gambling is a catch-22 situation anyway,' Noel said. 'The more you gamble, the more you get into debt; and the more you get into debt, the more you gamble. It goes on and on until you're backed into a corner with no way out.' When Brenda looked at him curiously, he shrugged. 'Not first-hand knowledge — I hate gambling — but an uncle of mine went down that route and finished up killing himself.' He turned back to his board and added Bradley Shelton to the list.

'I'm going to see if I can track Bradley down this morning,' Kevin said. 'He must be living somewhere and he's a pretty good suspect at the moment, but I doubt his mother had much money hidden away.'

Noel remembered the ring in his pocket and put it on Brenda's desk. 'Cassandra found this in her mother's handbag. It doesn't belong to Dora, so it probably belongs to Mary Shelton.' He held the ring up to the light. 'Cassandra says the stone is a good colour, whatever that means; it just looks green to me. Mrs Shelton's bedroom was ransacked, so Bradley might have been looking for it.' He sighed. 'All supposition, though, until we know something definite.'

'First of all, we need to place the son at the scene,' Kevin said. 'And with Mrs Shelton in a coma and Mrs Moon missing, that might be difficult.'

'Who called us out?' Noel asked.

Brenda picked up her notebook. 'An incident was called in by someone who refused to identify themselves.'

'Male or female?'

Brenda glanced at her notes and then looked up at Noel. 'Female.'

He raised an eyebrow. 'That's interesting. I was ready to arrest the son as soon as he turned up, but this puts a different light on things.'

'Do you think he had an accomplice?'

Noel looked over Brenda's shoulder at her handwritten notes. 'Not necessarily. You don't need a lot of strength to push someone down the stairs. A woman could have done it.'

'Dora Moon might have taken off because she was scared, and then phoned the incident in herself,' Kevin suggested tentatively. 'We know she was at the scene, and now she's missing. It looks a bit suspicious, doesn't it?'

'But she left her handbag behind with her phone in it,' Brenda said, 'and there's not a public landline anywhere in Norton. If she went under her own steam, she would have made sure she had her phone with her.' She gave Kevin a withering look. 'Besides, no woman takes off without her handbag, even if she's in a blind panic.'

Kevin held up his hands. 'I was just saying.'

Noel ignored them. 'I need to get hold of that recording.'

'It would have come in downstairs.' Kevin got to his feet. 'I'll go and get a copy.'

'I need the actual tape,' Noel told him, 'not a typed report of the conversation.'

'On my way.'

Noel was feeling the familiar rush of adrenaline. The case had gone from nothing to something in a few seconds. He loved it when that happened. 'How about the house-to-house interviews?' he asked Brenda.

She looked down at her notes again. 'Still going on, but Dave Mayrick paid a visit to the immediate neighbours yesterday evening. He said someone saw a car parked right up against the door of the Shelton house. Do you want me to call him?'

Noel picked up his phone. 'I'll do it.'

Mayrick came into Noel's office two

minutes later looking slightly apprehensive. 'Sir?'

'You called on one of Mrs Shelton's neighbours yesterday evening. She says she saw a car in the Shelton driveway. I need the relevant details.'

'It's all in my report, sir.'

'I know,' Noel said patiently, 'but I'd rather hear it first-hand so I can ask any questions that pop into my head.'

The young policeman went through his report word for word, exactly as it appeared on the form lying on Noel's desk. Noel waited until he had finished. 'So this woman lives next door to Mary Shelton and she saw a dark blue car parked up by the front door of the Shelton house?' Mayrick nodded. 'According to her, the car left about half an hour before the first officers arrived at the scene.' He thought for a moment. The drive was an in-and-out one. No gates, no fence or wall, just the driveway with a semicircle of grass between the entrance and exit. 'What direction was the car facing?'

Mayrick was silent. Eventually he said, 'Is that important, sir?'

Noel closed his eyes for a moment. He hadn't been at Norton long, and he didn't want to upset anyone at this early stage. 'Everything is important, Officer Mayrick. Mrs Shelton is in a coma. If she dies, this could become a murder investigation. However, at the time you spoke to Mrs . . . ' He looked down at the paper on his desk. ' . . . Blackwell, you didn't realise the significance of the question. Just remember to ask everything you can think of next time, whether it appears relevant or not.'

The young policeman had no sooner left than Kevin came back in carrying a cassette tape in a plastic evidence bag. 'I had to prise it out of their hot little hands,' he said with a grin. 'I'm supposed to tell you not to lose it because it might be important and needed as evidence.'

'Goodness me,' Brenda said. 'You would never have thought of that, would you, sir? Nice of them to remind you.' She opened a cupboard and pulled out an ancient cassette player. 'We don't use this often. I hope it still works.'

Noel could never understand why the police force hadn't gone digital, but he was too fired up with adrenaline to worry. The call had come in on the 101 non-emergency number, but luckily someone had realised it might be serious and sent out a patrol car to investigate. Mary Shelton was only lying at the bottom her stairs for a short time before the police arrived. According to the report on Brenda's desk, the front door was open when the police got to the house.

Kevin plugged in the machine and Noel slotted in the cassette. 'It'll tell you the time of each call,' Kevin said. 'Our one is at 3.16 p.m.'

Noel ran the tape through slowly, stopping every now and again to check the time frame. There were more calls than he would have believed possible for a small town. Non-emergency seemed to mean anything from a woman almost severing a finger with a kitchen knife, to misplaced spectacles.

The call he was waiting for was less distinct than he would have liked. It could very well have been Dora Moon, but he certainly couldn't swear to it. The line was muffled, the voice indistinct, and there was a lot of background noise.

'There's been an accident at number 6 Myrtle Close. Someone is badly hurt . . . perhaps dead . . . I'm . . . '

'Damn!' Noel let the tape run on a bit, but there was nothing until the next recorded message about a noisy neighbour. 'She was going to say something else.'

'So what stopped her?' Brenda turned off the machine and unplugged it from the wall. 'Was it Dora Moon? If someone took the phone away from her, she obviously wasn't alone.'

'It sounded like Dora, but I wouldn't swear to it in court. Whoever it was, she might have dropped the phone, or decided she'd already said enough.'

'She was in a car,' Kevin said. 'You could hear the road noise. Tyres on tarmac. Going at quite a lick, I reckon. It would be difficult to talk on a phone and drive at the same time when you're going at speed.'

'Get someone else to track down Bradley Shelton. Get hold of some photos to show around, use the one from the line-up if necessary, and find out if he's got any distinguishing marks, like tattoos or piercings. Also whether he takes any drugs, medicinal or otherwise. Most of that should be on his record.'

'He's got a couple of tattoos,' Brenda volunteered. 'I don't know what they are or where he got them, but I'm sure I can find out.'

'Good. If you don't have time to do it yourself, put someone else on it. We need to find Dora Moon. The longer she's out there, the less likely we are to find her alive. I'll chase up the hospital again, just in case she's turned up there.'

Noel knew he needed all the help he could get. He wondered what Hector Moon was actually doing. He had tried to find out what government department Hector actually worked for, but he'd hit stone walls every step of the way. The man was a complete enigma, but Noel was sure Hector Moon would do everything within his power to get his wife back safely.

4

Cass stared at her car in dismay. A good three inches of snow had given her Mini the appearance of a small igloo. Not a disaster as such, but it would still need to be cleared before she could go anywhere. Why, she wondered, do people keep the scraper to clear away the snow inside the car? To get to the scraper she had to open the car door, and to do that she had to find the handle.

Woollen gloves were probably not a good idea, so she took them off. The star sapphire on her finger shone with an inner fire, a gleam of brilliant light on a dull, wintery day. When her father gave the ring to her he told her the stone had magical qualities, but she had no idea what those magical qualities were, and at the moment she had no way of finding out. Perhaps if she could conjure up a bit more belief in the supernatural, she might have more success. As it was, she was pretty sure she'd have to rely on her scraper, which was still inside the snow-covered car. Half-closing her eyes, she pushed her bare hand into the snow, pulled the handle — and discovered the door was frozen shut.

Maybe it would be more sensible to give up and go back indoors. 'All I want,' she said with a sigh, 'is a spell to warm up the car so the snow falls off and the door opens. I don't think that's a lot to ask. So what do I have to do? Say a magic word or something, like abracadabra?'

It didn't happen immediately. She looked down at her hand as she felt the tingle of blood returning to her frozen fingers. Then the snow on the top of the car started to slip. She moved her feet out of the way just in time. Once the door handle was visible, she opened the car door and turned the key in the ignition. With the engine running and the heater on, the situation returned to a semblance of normality. Engine + heater + melting snow. Nothing weird about that.

Once she was out on the road, Cass began to realise that her original plan was a no-go. The holly bushes she had intended looking for were unrecognisable. Covered in a thick layer of snow, the shrubs could have been anything from a frozen camellia to a dead hydrangea. She also discovered there were a number of plants covered in red berries in the winter, but very few of them were actually holly.

Feeling defeated, she parked in a small shopping precinct and found a coffee shop she had been in several times before. The place was warm and not too crowded. It was still a little early in the morning for the regular clientele of elderly ladies wanting their coffee and cakes.

Cass walked up to the counter and ordered a latte. The girl who served her looked like a college student; skinny and pretty, with blonde hair scraped back into a ponytail and a sprinkle of freckles on her nose. 'Not nice out there,' the girl said as she poured the frothy mix into a glass mug. 'Glad I can walk here. It took my dad ages to scrape the snow off his car this morning. If I'd had to wait for him I'd have been late for work.'

'Yes, not nice at all,' Cass said. She wasn't quite ready to talk about the business of getting snow off cars. 'I haven't seen you before. Do you work here all the time, or is it a holiday job?'

'Only holidays. I'm still at college. Got another year to go.' She put the mug of coffee on a saucer and added a small foil-wrapped chocolate. 'Better eat that quick or it'll melt. They always do.'

Cass paid for her coffee and was about to move away when a tall, heavily built man came through the door in a flurry of snow. He glowered at Cass as if the weather was her fault, grabbed a packet of sandwiches, and fished in his

pocket for money. Freckles took the
hint and rushed to serve him. She took
his order for coffee and filled a
take-away container, hurrying to get his
change while he stamped his feet to get
the snow off. Obviously not trusting the
girl, he pushed the coins around on the
palm of his hand with one finger,
counting his change. Then, without so
much as a thank-you, he dropped the
money into his pocket and headed for
the door.

Cass stood transfixed, unable to
move, while her coffee mug jittered
noisily on the saucer.

'You all right?'

Cass realised the girl was looking at
her worriedly and shook her head to
clear it. 'Yes, thank you. I'm fine.'

When the man turned his hand over
to count his change, Cass had seen part
of a tattoo on his wrist. A tattoo that
looked exactly the same as the picture
Dora had drawn on the back of the
pigeon.

She took her coffee and walked to a

table by the window. As the man opened the door and left the shop, she frantically rubbed the window to clear a space in the condensation, hoping to see him get into a car, but he walked away up the street and she lost sight of him. She had been sure he would have a car, and then she could have made a note of the registration number. A moment later a car went past the window, moving much too fast for the condition of the road. Cass couldn't see the registration number, but the car was a dark colour. Maybe blue or black.

She had no idea what to do next. She had been standing beside the man who had probably kidnapped her mother, and she had let him walk away. She should have called the police — called Noel and had the man arrested — but she had no idea how she could she have kept him in the café until the police arrived. She finished her coffee and went back to the counter.

'Are you feeling better?' the girl asked. 'You looked as if you were going to faint or something.'

'It was just the cold,' Cass said, trying to sound reassuring. 'It took me a long time to clear my car this morning.' Not as long as it might have done, she thought, but a little white lie never hurt anyone. 'That man, the one who came in for a take-out coffee, do you know him?'

The girl giggled. 'Wasn't he in a mood? Late for work, I reckon. He comes in here some mornings for a coffee, but I don't know who he is.' She looked at Cass curiously. 'Why are you asking?'

'I thought I recognised him,' Cass said. Lying was fast becoming a habit. 'Someone my mother knows. But it doesn't matter. Like you said, he was in a really bad mood. I didn't want to talk to him.'

'If he comes in again, do you want me to tell him you asked after him?'

Cass shook her head. That was the last thing she wanted. 'No, thank you. I could easily have been mistaken.'

Outside, a flurry of snow hit her in the face and she was thankful to get into her still-warm car. Rather than phone Noel, she decided to drive to the police station and tell him what had happened. She kept thinking of things she should have done, like take a photo of the man on her phone. When she was standing at the counter she had thought of taking a photo of the tattoo, but in retrospect that might not have been a good idea.

It took longer to drive to the police station than normal. As is usual in England, an inch of snow had brought traffic almost to a standstill even though the bad weather had been forecast a week ago. The roads were clear, but dirty grey sludge still lined the gutters and lay in slushy heaps on the pathways. The few pedestrians were hunched down, heads tucked inside a variety of scarves and turned-up collars. Cass decided she needed a pair of leather gloves. She couldn't hold the steering wheel in her woollen ones and her hands were freezing. The heater in the old Mini had trouble pushing any warmth further up than her knees and the windscreen was continually misting up. She sighed; maybe a new car was in order.

She asked for Noel at the reception desk and was shown straight up to his office. He greeted her at the door, tall and brooding, his dark hair always a shade too long. A modern-day Heathcliff.

'Come inside, Cass. You look frozen.' He shut the door into the outer office and pulled out a chair for her. 'Sit down and get warm. Have you heard from Dora?'

She shook her head. 'No, and I'm scared for her, Noel, but that wasn't what I came to see you about. I think I saw the man who took her.' She explained about her encounter in the coffee shop, stumbling over her words until he told her to slow down. 'And then I noticed his tattoo.'

'Tattoo?'

'Yes. On the underside of his wrist. The same as the picture on the bird. Have you still got my drawing?' He opened a file on his desk, took out a copy of her drawing and handed it to her.

'Yes, that's what I saw. The tattoo was half-hidden by his sleeve, but it looked exactly the same as this.'

'So you couldn't see all the tattoo, just part of it?'

'Yes, and I think that's why I recognised it.' She got up from the chair and walked to the window, looking down at the street below. 'I should have stopped him, shouldn't I? My mother might be home by now if I'd done something to stop him leaving.'

He gently took her shoulders and led her back to the chair. 'You could be mistaken about the tattoo, and you couldn't have stopped him leaving. If you'd tried to say anything to him, he would have been warned. Doing something like that might have put your mother's life in danger.' He squatted down in front of her and she could see the glint of silver in his grey eyes. 'You did exactly the right thing, and we'll get her back, Cass, I promise.'

She managed a half-smile. 'I just felt so useless. He was there in front of me, and I couldn't do anything.'

Noel got to his feet. 'Brenda told me that Bradley Shelton has a few tattoos, but he's only five-eight and on the skinny side. We've got a description of him that was only taken last year, so unless he's grown several inches and put on a lot of weight, the man you saw in the café wasn't Bradley.'

Cass frowned. 'Does Bradley Shelton have a picture of a holly leaf on his wrist?'

'I shouldn't imagine so. Not unless one of the local tattoo parlours is doing a discount on holly leaves, and I wouldn't think that would be a particularly popular design. It's a bit seasonal, isn't it? Not something you'd want on your body for life.'

She thought she detected a note of scepticism in his voice. 'I wasn't mistaken, Noel.'

He sighed. 'I believe you, Cass, but we have no way of catching up with this guy. He could be anywhere. If he has Dora stashed away somewhere, or knows where she is, there's nothing we can do about it at the moment.'

Cass's mobile phone rang and she fumbled in her pocket to get it out. For one moment she thought it might be her mother, but then she saw Liz Portman's name on the screen. She gave Noel an apologetic look and answered the call. Liz was her best friend, and she realised guiltily that Liz had no idea her mother was missing.

'I can't talk now, Liz. I'm with Noel at the police station.'

'Is she home yet?'

'How did you know?' Cass didn't wait for an answer. 'No, she's still missing. Someone took her. I think she's still alive, but I don't know where she is, and Noel isn't getting anywhere, either.' She glanced across at the detective. 'I must go now, but can I meet you for lunch?'

Liz wouldn't have time to chat, either. She was a nurse at the local hospital. 'It'll have to be late. Two o'clock at the usual place, and I'll only be able to spare half an hour.'

'See you at two, then.' Cass hung up, glad she would be able to spend a little time with her friend. Liz lived her life firmly grounded in reality, unlike the rest of the people Cass knew.

Noel looked at his watch. 'Have you got time to work with the police artist? We might be able to get a reasonable likeness of the man you saw while his face is fresh in your mind.'

Cass spent nearly an hour with the artist, apologising several times for her poor memory. The trouble was, once she had seen the tattoo, she hadn't really noticed anything else about the man. In the end, they had a face in front of them, but Cass wasn't sure it looked anything like the man in the café. She felt she had done the best she could, and she was almost late for her meeting with Liz.

The two friends always met at the same pub for lunch; sometimes just for a coffee if that was all Liz could manage. She worked shifts, so she was never sure when she would be free.

'How did you know about my mother?' Cass asked. They had ordered sandwiches at the bar to save time, and they both had mugs of coffee in front of them.

'I saw Mrs Shelton on the ward, and then a couple of policemen came round asking questions. One of them said the witch from the big house had gone missing.' Liz pulled a face. 'I sort of guessed who they were talking about. What happened, Cass?'

'I have no idea. My mother went to visit Mary and didn't come home when she said she would, so I went looking for her. When I got to the house the police were there already. They found Mary at the bottom of the stairs unconscious, but there was no sign of Dora. She was missing all last night.' Cass swallowed hard. 'I phoned Hector and he came straight away. If anyone can find her, he can.'

'But you think she's OK?'

'I keep telling myself I'd know if anything bad had happened to her; but I've got to believe that, haven't I?'

Cass wondered if she was kidding herself, but she had to trust her instincts. Dora might be injured, but Cass knew in her heart her mother was still alive. She didn't mention the bird to Liz. She had no idea why they all believed the marks on the pigeon's feathers were a drawing sent by Dora, but they all did. Cass had a feeling Liz would be a little more realistic.

'I guess you already know Mrs Shelton is in an induced coma,' Liz said. 'They did another scan this morning and the tiny bleed they saw in her head has stopped, so they'll try and wake her up tomorrow or the next day. Once she's awake, she should be able to tell us exactly what happened. That's if the injury hasn't done any permanent damage to her brain.'

'We need to find my mother before then. She can't spend any more time out in the cold.' Cass shivered. 'If it snows much more we won't be able to carry on looking for her.' She couldn't tell Liz about the man she had seen in the café without going into details about the bird. In the crowded pub with people talking and laughing around her, the whole episode seemed surreal. She had grown up with magic, but now she was beginning to think they were all going quietly mad.

Her mother was missing, that was a fact, and all the talk of spells and magic wouldn't get her back. Like Hector said, it was all down to methodical police work. The problem was, Hector might have said something like that, but Cass knew he didn't mean a word of it. He had said it to put her mind at rest and stop her doing anything dangerous. Now he was off somewhere doing his own thing — and that was exactly what she intended to do, too.

Liz promised a regular progress report on Mrs Shelton, and they both braved the still-falling snow to get to their respective cars. Liz had to get back to the hospital, and Cass headed in the direction the man had taken when he left the café. There was always a chance she might see him on the street somewhere. A very small chance, considering the weather, but a chance all the same. For some ridiculous reason she half-expected to see her mother, wrapped in her pashmina, battling her way through the snow.

She didn't see her mother, but she did drive past the entrance to one of Norton's three night clubs. She was in a rough part of town, and the outside of the club was in keeping with the area. The windows on to the street were covered with blinds and the chipped wooden door was closed. Cass slowed her car and pulled into the kerb. The place looked deserted, but Cass could see a chink of light beneath one of the blinds.

She sat in her car for a moment, wondering whether to get out or not. It wasn't the look of the club that had stopped her in her tracks; it was the club name painted on a board over the door.

'The Bat Club' stood out boldly in black letters. Next to the name was a logo — a line-drawing of a bat in flight. From where Cass was sitting, the drawing looked very much like two holly leaves joined in the middle.

5

She took her phone out of her bag and then put it back again. If she phoned Noel, he would have to show his badge before he asked any questions. She thought she could do better. At least people didn't clam up as soon as they looked at her. Not usually. She would just be a woman asking about a man with a tattoo. For all anyone knew, she might be the man's ex-wife.

She locked the car when she got out, but she took her handbag with her so she'd have her phone handy if she needed it. If there were lights on inside the building, then someone was home. She looked at her watch. She had a couple of hours before it got completely dark — time enough to have a quick word with someone inside. The man with the tattoo must have something to do with the club, and connecting the dots meant he also had something to do with Dora and the pigeon.

She got out of her car and walked to the door. Expecting it to be locked, she tried the handle, almost losing her balance when the door swung inwards without any warning. She found herself in a small lobby, facing an unattended desk. The outside door closed behind her of its own volition, leaving her in semi-darkness. She was about to beat a hasty retreat when a door behind the desk opened and a man appeared. He was of indeterminate age, small and rat-like, with black framed glasses perched near the end of his nose. His ears were too big for his face and his mouth too small. Once upon a time he might have been an adorable infant, but if he had been her baby she would have handed him back.

'I've been told to fetch you. The Man wants to see you.'

It was all so Hollywood-movie, she wanted to laugh. Whoever 'The Man' was, he'd probably seen her drive up on an outside camera, and now he was watching her on another camera mounted on the wall above the desk. She still thought it might be a good idea to leave right now and phone Noel, but her curiosity had been tweaked, and she wanted to find out all she could about the club.

By the time they reached a door at the end of a long, dark corridor, Cass was starting to feel a little nervous, and her ring had picked up her vibes. It felt almost uncomfortably warm on her finger, the star in the centre of the sapphire flashing so brightly she could see it through her woollen glove.

The little man opened the door and almost pushed her into the room, shuffling back up the corridor before she realised he had left her on her own. Someone was inside the room, standing in shadow. A tall, lean man wearing a black suit, his shirt cuffs showing an inch of white below the sleeves of his jacket. That was all she could see clearly, apart from a diamond ring on his finger which flashed as brightly as her sapphire. This, presumably, was The Man.

As he stepped forward into the light, she got a better look at him. He had very pale skin, but the rest of him was dark. His hair was jet-black and his eyes the same colour, with no distinction between the iris and the pupil. With his black suit he should have looked like an undertaker, but instead he looked like Count Dracula. Lean and handsome maybe, but also deadly. Cass had thought all this was a bit of a joke a few minutes ago, but not anymore. A primordial fear sent a trickle of ice coursing through her body.

He smiled at her. 'The club is closed until eight tonight, but the bar is open all day. May I get you a drink?'

She wanted to run. Every bone in her body was telling her to run. She shouldn't be here on her own, she realised that now. She should have phoned Noel and waited for him to arrive. Her heart rate had escalated to such an extent she felt dizzy. She brought it back down with a conscious effort. She didn't have panic attacks. They might happen to other people, but not to her. Without really thinking what she was doing, she took off her gloves and dropped them in her bag.

He saw the ring on her finger and smiled at her, showing very white teeth. 'Hello, Casandra.'

'How do you know my name?' The words came out at barely a whisper. She cleared her throat. Never show fear. Her mother had taught her that. 'Have we met before?'

'Maybe in our dreams, but never in the physical world. I recognised your ring. It's very distinctive. Your father told me he had given it to you.'

'You know Hector?' She tried very hard not to sound as surprised as she felt, but her voice squeaked a little.

'I know him well. He talks about you often. My name is Lucien, by the way. Come into the bar and let me buy you a drink.'

She could refuse and tell him she had somewhere more important to be, somewhere much more important than having a drink with him, but she had a feeling that might be a mistake. Besides, like he said, he knew her father, otherwise he wouldn't have known about her ring. Somewhat reassured by her own logic, she smiled back. 'Thank you, that would be nice.'

The room he took her into was well lit and warm, immediately calming her remaining fears. A few men were already having a lunchtime drink, most of them drinking beer, but none of them looked like the man from the café. A wood-burning stove sent out waves of welcoming heat and the tables scattered about the room gleamed with recent polish.

Cass decided she had been letting her imagination play tricks on her. She gratefully accepted the glass of wine Lucien put in front of her, refusing to listen to her inner voice muttering about the possibility of poison. She needed a drink, and there was nothing to suggest this man had anything sinister in mind.

'I won't flatter myself that you came here solely to meet me, Cassandra. I doubt your father would have mentioned me to you. We weren't on the best of terms last time we met, but that is by the by.' He pulled out a chair for her and then sat down on the opposite side of the table. 'So what can I do for you?'

He had thrown her into confusion again. He might know Hector, but it didn't sound as if they were friends. If she wanted to keep her mother's abduction and the business with the pigeon to herself, she had to make up a story quickly. The black eyes boring into her skull told her she had better make it sound good even if it was a lie.

'I was in a coffee shop this morning and a man left his change on the counter. The weather was atrocious and he was obviously in a hurry. Anyway, I happened to notice he had a tattoo on his wrist, and when I drove past here I realised it was the same as your logo. I thought you might know who he is.'

It sounded plausible to her, but Lucien was smiling at her in such a deprecating way she was beginning to think she must have said something stupid.

'The Bat Club has almost one hundred members, Cassandra, and most of them will have the club logo tattooed on them somewhere. It is a temporary mark done with a new type of ink that lasts six months. Once the mark disappears, our members know it is time to pay their next membership fee. I find the tattoo works better than a membership card. For one thing, it can't be lost.' He looked at her glass. 'Is the wine to your liking?'

'Yes, thank you.' She wanted to leave, but she had to finish her wine first and leave quietly, not run screaming for the door like a maniac. 'How long have you been open?'

'Only a month, but the business is

going well. We have a roulette wheel and several different card games, all of it perfectly legitimate, I assure you. We put out some flyers before we opened and got a good response.'

She managed to finish her wine without gulping it, and stood up. 'I must be going, but thank you for your time.'

'Of course.' He stood up as well, seeming to tower over her. 'I'm sorry I was unable to help you. Our members can be quite touchy about their privacy; they rely on our absolute discretion, so I wouldn't be able to tell you anything about this man, even if I knew who he was.'

He reached for her hand, but changed his mind at the last moment, giving her a little bow instead. Cass saw he was staring at her ring, which was flashing like the evening star.

'Please tell Hector I admire his choice of jewellery.' His voice reminded her of dark treacle, thick and sticky. 'The ring he gave you is one of a kind.

If I were you, I would take great care of it.'

All Cass wanted to do now was make her escape. The room had suddenly become claustrophobic and the lights seemed to have dimmed, leaving dark shadows lurking in the corners. She picked up her bag, wondering why her mouth was so dry and hoping the wine hadn't really been poisoned. By the time she reached the outside door, she was beginning to understand the phrase 'abject terror'.

Lucien reached past her, and for a moment she thought he was going to open the door, but instead he leaned against it, blocking her exit.

'Don't forget to tell your father you came to see me, Cassandra, and tell him you took wine with me. That will amuse him. Also, give my best wishes to your mother. I hear she is out and about again after her breakdown. I'm sorry you have to leave so soon. If you come here again, I'll make sure you stay longer.'

Why did that sound like a threat? she wondered. He released his hold on the door and held it open for her. She stepped out into the cold and was surprised to see the world looked completely normal. Her car was parked at the kerb, the snow had stopped falling, and on the other side of the street a couple were walking a dog. She fumbled with her keys and eventually managed to start the engine and drive away.

She considered driving to the police station again, but she knew Noel was busy, and he would begin to think she was stalking him. Interrupting him by telephoning would be just as bad. Anything she had learned, which wasn't very much, she could tell him later. Now her father was home, there was no need for Noel to stay the night, but she hoped he would call in before he went home to his flat.

She pulled into a layby as soon as she was out of sight of the club and phoned Liz. At least she could find out about Mary Shelton.

Liz said Mary had been taken off the drugs and was slowly coming out of her induced coma. The hospital had put a ban on visitors until tomorrow. Even members of the police force had been told to stay away. Liz said she would do what she could, but Mary was in the ICU, and out of bounds.

By the time Cass got back to the house and parked her car it was fully dark, and she realised her mother would be spending another night somewhere away from home and probably in danger. The outside light was on, and for a moment she felt a surge of hope. Perhaps her mother was home. But then she realised her father had probably turned the light on.

She was surprised to find the kitchen warm and smelling of something delicious. Tobias was asleep on his usual chair and Hector was sprawled out on the sofa reading a paper. It was all so domestic-looking, and all so different from what Cass was used to, she wondered for a moment if she was in the wrong house.

Hector looked up from his paper, a frown on his face. 'Where have you been?'

She blinked. 'Sorry?' She was surprised he had to ask. Shouldn't a warlock know these things?

'Don't look so innocent, Cassandra. Your mother is still missing, in spite of all my efforts, and I'm hearing rumours of dark magic. This isn't an ordinary kidnapping.'

She immediately felt guilty. She should have realised he would worry; his wife was missing and his daughter was late home. Even so, he had no right to treat her as if she was a child.

'Are you suggesting there's magic involved in this?' she said. 'How could there be? Mary and her son have never had anything to do with witchcraft.'

'That's as may be.' Hector got to his feet and poured red wine into two glasses from a bottle on the table. 'Take your coat off and sit down. I put a casserole in the oven two hours ago. It'll be ready shortly, but until it is, you can sit down and tell me where you've been.'

She had no idea what government department her father worked for, but it obviously had something to do with interrogation. If she didn't talk, he'd probably try water-boarding her next. She slipped off her coat and gloves and then pulled off her boots. The heat of the kitchen was like a warm bath, soothing and relaxing. She was sure that was exactly what Hector had been aiming for. The red wine was just an added ploy to make her even more talkative.

She slid into a chair opposite him and picked up her glass, remembering this was her second glass of wine and she needed to keep her wits about her. Hector was too clever by far. 'I met an acquaintance of yours today.'

Hector greeted this information with a slight frown, and she wondered if he ever let his guard down and showed genuine emotion. But she understood the frown; she was sure he could count his acquaintances on the fingers of one hand.

'And who would that be?'

'A man called Lucien. I didn't ask his second name because he said you knew him well. Tall, with black hair and very white skin. A bit spooky, actually.'

Hector sat back in his chair and sipped his wine, his expression unreadable. 'He calls himself all manner of things, depending on how he feels at the time. Sometimes he goes by the name of Loki, or maybe even Lucifer. He's not actually the devil, but he likes to think he is. If you met him in his own habitat, Cassandra, you're lucky he let you leave. Tell me exactly what happened, and try not to leave anything out because it could be very important.'

She had no intention of leaving anything out. Hector had just made a bad day even worse. She started with the encounter in the café and her visit to Noel, which gave her an opportunity to explain why she had stopped outside the Bat Club in the first place. Hector seemed barely interested until she got to the part about the club and her meeting with Lucien.

'So you actually sat and had a glass of wine with him? What were you thinking of, Cassandra? Do you normally walk into a strange gaming club and drink wine with the proprietor?'

When she thought about it, no, she didn't. So what had made her do it this time? She realised she had been manipulated all the way. First a scary bit, dark corridors and a creepy employee, then relief because everything seemed fairly normal in the bar, which made her drop her guard. Then another scary bit, much worse this time, which left her so relieved to get out into the normal world she rushed home to tell Daddy.

'He said you told him you'd given me the star sapphire ring. That's why I trusted him.' It helped to dump the blame back on Hector. It wasn't her fault the damn ring had been flashing like a neon sign.

'I told him so he would know you had something to keep you safe, but that ring can only do so much. You have to be aware of the dangers, Cassandra. I've told you that before. You can't rely on anything or anyone to keep you completely safe from evil. In the end, you have to rely on yourself.'

'I can't be aware of the dangers if I don't know what's going on. Who is this man? And why should I be afraid of him? I need to know who and what to look out for.'

Hector sighed. 'Your mother told me you could be difficult. You never take anything at face value, do you Cassandra? You have to know all the whys and wherefores.'

'That philosophy has kept me safe up to now,' she said tartly. 'I didn't need a magic ring. Not until you decided to come back home.'

The little upturn at the side of her father's mouth wasn't caused by humour, Cass decided. 'That isn't quite true,' he said evenly, obviously holding back his temper with some difficulty. 'Your mother called me back because she thought you were in danger.'

'I wasn't in nearly as much danger then as I am now. My mother is missing, Mary Shelton is hanging on to life by a thread, and I spent the afternoon with the devil. You know what, Father? Life has been just peachy since you came back.' She suddenly had an unexpected compulsion to burst into tears, and Hector knew it; she could see it in his eyes. He turned his back on her and walked to the stove.

'The casserole is ready. Find a place at the table, Cassandra, and pour yourself another glass of wine. I can see you had a bad day, but not all of it was my fault.'

She did as she was told, feeling a little stab of guilt. 'I just want to know what's going on. I can't keep myself safe if I don't have all the pieces of the puzzle.'

Hector filled her plate with food and she suddenly realised how hungry she was. The casserole had most likely been made by her mother and frozen, but he had taken the trouble to heat it up and supply the wine. There was even warm bread and a tub of butter. He could have eaten earlier and left her to fend for herself.

'I don't have all the pieces of the puzzle myself,' he said, topping up her wineglass. 'But Lucien is a bad character. I'm worried that he's the one who has taken your mother.'

Cass shook her head, her mouth too full to speak. She swallowed hurriedly. 'No, he made a point of asking how Dora was. He said to give her his love. I'm sure he doesn't know she's missing.'

'He might have been toying with you. He's well known for his trickery.'

She shook her head again. 'No, he wasn't looking for my reaction. He thought sending Dora his love would wind you up.' An unwelcome thought suddenly crossed her mind. 'How well does my mother know him?'

This time Hector's smile was genuine. 'Not that well. She only met him once. She wasn't scared of him, but she didn't like him much. He dresses like a fop and behaves like an idiot, and that disguises how dangerous he really is. He wants to rule the universe, Cassandra, and he'll do anything it takes to achieve that.'

Cass pushed her plate to one side, surprised to find she had eaten everything. 'How about the picture my mother sent to Noel? Lucien or Loki or whatever you call him must be involved. It was a picture of his club logo.'

'It was a picture of a tattoo that everyone who is a club member has on their wrist. But the club is still implicated in some way. And Lucien Constantine is here in Norton for something. He opened that club for a reason. A reason that has nothing to do with gaming. Besides, you said the club was a bit sleazy. That's not Lucien's style. He's got some ulterior motive; and until we discover what he's really after, we'll remain in the dark.'

6

Noel arrived as Cass was about to go to bed. It was barely ten o'clock, but she was exhausted. He came in the back door stamping his feet and banging his gloved hands together.

'It's freezing out there, literally. Colder than a penguin's nether region.' He gratefully took the shot of single malt Hector handed to him. 'I've been to the hospital and I managed to have a word with the doctor. They're bringing Mary out of her coma tonight but no one can see her until tomorrow morning, and then it's only a select few. I've been trying to trace other family members, but since her mother died, it seems Bradley is all she has.'

'That's sad,' Cass said. 'I'll visit as soon as they let me. She'll need some support when she comes out of hospital.' She looked at her father. 'Is my mother still alive? If she is, she must be somewhere she has shelter and food, or she wouldn't have survived this long.'

'I'm sure she's still alive, but I don't know where she is, so I can't tell you how long she'll remain alive if we don't find her soon. Tell Noel about your adventures while I get him something to eat.'

'I don't need you to feed me,' Noel protested. 'I can get something on the way home.'

Hector pulled on an oven glove and turned round, his hand on the casserole lid. 'Are you hungry right now?' When Noel nodded, he laughed and spooned stew into a bowl, adding a chunk of still-warm bread. 'It seems we have a visitor from the dark side here in Norton. Cassandra had the misfortune to call on him this afternoon, but she got away safely.'

Noel frowned at her. 'Why were you out of the house? You were supposed to stay here and work on your jewellery.'

She smiled at him sweetly. 'I very rarely do what I'm supposed to, Noel. You should know that by now. If you want me to tell you what happened, sit down and be quiet.'

The sympathetic look her father sent Noel meant the men were ganging up on her. She didn't add anything to her story. Noel wanted facts, so she tried to keep it as simple as possible, leaving out the spooky atmosphere of the Bat Club and playing down her own feeling of terror. She knew Noel would go and visit the club to meet Lucien in person and couldn't wait to see how he liked the experience.

He listened to her in relative quiet, only stopping her once or twice to ask questions, mainly about the inside of the club and the layout of the rooms. She gave him a detailed description of the club owner, but she couldn't begin to explain the aura of evil that surrounded the man. She didn't understand it herself.

Noel was quiet for a few moments

after she finished, then he turned to look at Hector. 'So you know this man? I take it he's not actually a reincarnation of the devil, so who the hell is he?'

Hector waved the wine bottle enquiringly. When both Noel and Cassandra declined, he topped up his own glass. 'He usually goes by the name Lucien Constantine. I know for a fact he has a passport and a driving licence in that name. He dabbles in anything that'll make him money or gain him power. His main incentive is power. Like I said, he wants to rule the universe.'

'I've met a few power-hungry men in my time,' Noel said, 'but power enough to rule the world is usually enough. Even Adolph Hitler would have been satisfied with world domination. I think control of the universe is even outside NATO's jurisdiction.' The frown lines between Noel's dark brows deepened. 'So what, I wonder, is Lucien Constantine doing in Norton?'

★　★　★

Noel was in his office by 7.30 the following morning. He had gratefully eaten Hector's stew and then left Cass in the safe hands of her father. He needed a good night's sleep if he was going to confront Lucien Constantine at the Bat Club, but before he paid the man a visit, a thorough online check was in order.

Lucien Constantine did indeed have a hand in a number of pies. He had been arrested on two occasions, but easily bought his way out of trouble with a clever lawyer. He had gaming clubs in several medium-sized towns scattered about the country, and Noel noticed his name had been linked with extortion. He encouraged compulsive gamblers to get further into debt and then forced them to do his bidding. Noel added a couple of printed pages of notes to a folder and dropped it into a drawer in his desk.

There were still a number of questions with no probable answers. From what Hector had said, Constantine was in Norton for a reason, and Noel needed to find out what that reason was. He also wanted to know what the Bat Club had to do with Pandora Moon's disappearance. Apart from the fact that she was Cassandra's mother, Noel liked the little witch.

Whoever had ransacked Mary Shelton's house had been searching for a particular item, possibly the emerald ring. Whatever actually happened, Dora had been witness to something that made her a threat. One of the reasons he didn't think she was in immediate danger was because she could have been killed at the house. There was no need to go to the trouble of removing her from the scene of the crime. He could only assume the perpetrator thought he had killed her when he pushed her down the stairs. Of course, the villain could be a woman, but he didn't think so. His number-one suspect was Mrs Shelton's son, Bradley. Whoever did the searching knew the object they were looking for was in her room.

Noel looked at his watch. He had no idea how early the Bat Club opened, but probably not until near lunchtime, and the owner was likely to arrive even later. Cass had found Constantine at the club in the afternoon, so Noel would try and arrive at about the same time. First he had to visit the hospital, where he hoped to find the injured woman fully awake and able to fill in some of the blank spaces in his investigation.

The half-thawed snow had frozen again during the night and it took him all of ten minutes to clean the ice from his windscreen. The sky was a thick, murky grey, threatening more snow, but for the moment it was just bitterly cold. He thought again of Dora Moon, and how anxious Cass must be, but he had to put all the stray thoughts out of his mind or he wouldn't be able to do his job.

There was already a police officer stationed outside Mary's room. She was

Noel's only witness, and the only person who might be able to shed light on where her son was hiding out. Bradley Shelton's disappearance was too convenient. There had been no sign of a break-in, so whoever called on Mary on that cold winter's afternoon had most likely been let into the house via the front door. Her son's fingerprints were all over the place, but that was to be expected. The only fresh new fingerprints found at the house belonged to Dora Moon.

At least the hospital was warm, almost too warm after the cold outside. Noel introduced himself at the reception desk and a nurse took him up to the first floor of the hospital. Mary had been moved from the ICU to a private room with round-the-clock care. She was fully conscious and talking, but he had been warned not to tire her out and was given a maximum of just ten minutes.

She was propped up on pillows and gave him a weak smile when he came into the room.

'My name is Noel Raven. I'm the detective inspector investigating your fall.' He moved closer to the bed and sat on the only chair. The woman looked pale and bruised. A white bandage covered most of her head, but her eyes were bright and she looked surprisingly robust for a woman who had been near death a few days ago.

'I know who you are, Detective. They told me you were coming to ask me some questions.'

Noel had a funny feeling this wasn't going to be as easy as it appeared, and he didn't have time to play around. 'Your mother's bedroom was ransacked, Mrs Shelton, so we know someone was looking for something. Can you tell me who broke into your house and pushed you down the stairs?'

Her eyes were black and blue from the injury to her head, and one of them was half-closed. 'I had a friend over for afternoon tea and I was going to show her something. I couldn't find it and I was in a hurry. No one pushed me. I fell down the stairs because I wasn't looking where I was going.'

'The doctor told me your injuries look as if you were propelled down the stairs, rather than just losing your footing.'

'I tripped and fell head first. I was in a hurry to get back to my friend, who I'd left downstairs on her own.'

'So if we talk to Dora Moon she will be able to confirm your story.'

Just for a moment a flash of alarm crossed the woman's face, but it was gone almost immediately. 'I'm sure she will. Dora Moon has a daughter who's a jeweller. I went upstairs to find a ring I wanted Cassandra Moon to look at; I was hoping she could reset it for me. That's why I was upstairs; I was looking for the ring. My mother died recently, and the ring is the only thing I have left that belonged to my father. He died when I was just a child. If you talk to Dora, can you please ask her to keep the ring safe for me until I come out of hospital?'

Noel was now positive Bradley Shelton had ransacked his grandmother's bedroom looking for the ring, and then pushed his mother down the stairs. There was no other reason for the woman to lie about what had happened to her.

'I'm afraid we can't ask Dora Moon anything. She's been missing for two days and nights. She's somewhere out in the bitter cold all on her own and we need to find her. We think your son is involved in some way, but we can't talk to him because he's missing as well.' He leaned forward so he could look straight into Mary Shelton's shocked face. 'I need your help, Mary, or Dora might die. If your son took her from your house, where would he go?'

The woman gave him a look that said she would never hand her son over to the police, and then she covered her face with her hands and started to cry — loud, stricken sobs that had hospital staff rushing into the room. A nurse hurried to Mary's bedside and a man in a white coat faced Noel furiously.

'You have to leave! Right now! I should never have agreed to let you talk to Mrs Shelton. Do you people have no soul? This woman was attacked in her own home, and now you come here and harass her in her hospital bed. You should be ashamed of yourself.'

'I just need an answer to my last question,' Noel said desperately. 'A life may be in danger.'

'A life *is* in danger. You put this woman's life in danger just by being in her room.' The man in the white coat held open the door leading out into the corridor. 'I'm asking you to leave right now, or I will have you thrown out.'

Noel had a feeling the man would make good his threat, so he left as requested. He had seen the look on Mary's face before she started making enough noise to wake the dead. Whatever Bradley did, he was still her only son, and she would never betray him.

He was getting more and more

worried about Pandora Moon and more and more frustrated with the lack of leads. A search of the area had been unproductive and, apart from the fact that a car had been parked outside Mary's house, there was nothing to tie Bradley to the crime scene. Bradley was out of work. He had been staying with various friends for the past few weeks, dossing down with whoever would have him, so where could he take Dora?

Noel had a quick lunch in a nearby pub and headed for the Bat Club. He was curious about the man he was going to meet. Hector had described Lucien Constantine as the epitome of evil, and Noel knew Cassandra had been playing down her experience at the club. He wished, just for once, she would do what she was told, but he knew there was no chance of that. He worried about her, and he didn't like worrying about people; it distracted him from doing his job. His grandmother had told him that responsibility made you stronger, but he knew from experience it didn't always work that way. Constantly worrying about someone made you vulnerable, and now he wasn't only worrying about Cass, he was worrying about her mother as well.

From the outside, the club looked more or less as he had expected: a typical, slightly down-market gambling club, the facade a little tired and grubby-looking. A couple of signs offered a free £50 opening bet and one free drink per session. There was also a half-dead plant in a pot and a door that looked as if it had been kicked a few times.

Noel got out of his car and walked slowly towards the club entrance. The door was unlocked and open a few inches. He thought of the spider and the fly, but he still pushed the door fully open and walked inside.

He couldn't wait to meet this man. The man who'd scared Cassandra. She didn't scare easily, and she would never admit to it, but he'd seen it in her eyes. It didn't surprise him all that much to find Lucien Constantine waiting for him just inside the door.

'Detective Inspector, how nice to meet you.'

Noel didn't answer immediately. He had stepped inside the bat cave, and he wanted to make sure the exit was clear in his head. When he turned his attention back to Constantine, he was surprised to find the man wasn't as imposing as he had expected. Constantine looked like a typical club owner: a little over the top in his dress, his smile a little too white, and his voice a little too smooth. But then Noel looked into the man's eyes. Cold and dark in a dead white face. Constantine might be a master of disguise, but he couldn't hide the snakelike slither of something evil just beneath the surface.

Noel had seen more than he was supposed to, and Constantine's expression changed. Gone was the benign gambling-club owner, and instead Noel faced something that was only human on the surface. Beneath the smooth exterior a chimera lurked.

'Nice to meet you, too, Mr Constantine. You were obviously expecting me.'

The white smile was back. 'Of course. I hate to be taken by surprise.'

It was Noel's turn to smile. He could play this game just as well. It was part of his job. 'I'm sure you do. Surprise visits can be a bit tricky.'

He moved further into the room, forcing Constantine to move back a pace. He felt he ought to be scared — intimidated at the very least — but instead he felt exhilarated. If it came to a fight, he was pretty sure he could take this man on and win.

Constantine lost his smile. 'I assume you wanted to ask me some questions. Shall we move into another room where it will be more comfortable?'

Spiders and flies again. Noel shook his head. 'Here will be just fine. I won't keep you long. I'm trying to track down the whereabouts of one of your members, a young man called Bradley Shelton. He has a tattoo of a bat on his wrist, which is what brought me to you.'

'As I am sure you are aware, detective, all our club members have a tattoo on their hand — a semi-permanent picture of our logo which lasts about six months.'

'Do you have an address for Bradley?'

'I do, but whether I pass this information on or not is another matter. Can I ask why you want to know Bradley Shelton's whereabouts? Has he done something wrong?'

Noel had no intention of telling Constantine about Dora Moon's abduction. The man might already know — but then again, he might not.

'I'm afraid I can't tell you that.'

'Then I'm afraid I can't divulge Bradley's whereabouts.' The white smile was back. 'Particularly not to a police officer.' He held up a hand imperiously when he saw Noel was about to speak. 'But as it happens, I don't want to cause any friction between myself and the local police force. Bradley Shelton is staying here, at the club, until he finds somewhere more permanent to live.'

Noel tried not to show his surprise. A million conflicting thoughts raced through his head. Had he been completely wrong all this time — looking in the wrong place and giving the real perpetrator time to get away; putting Dora's life in danger? 'May I speak with him?'

'Not without a warrant.'

'Then perhaps you could inform Mr Shelton that his mother is in hospital. She's been taken off the critical list, but she's still very ill. Tell him she's been asking for her son.'

'How very sweet. She must care about him a great deal. Did Bradley's mother have an accident of some sort?'

Noel had a feeling Constantine was laughing at him. He wanted more information, but he knew it wouldn't be forthcoming. He was in a situation now where he was going to have to reevaluate everything he thought he knew and go through the whole thing again right from the beginning. If Bradley hadn't taken Dora, then who had, and where was she now? Then again, there was always the possibility that Lucien Constantine was just toying with him, and nothing he said contained a shred of truth.

'I'm afraid I can't tell you that either, but I must let you get on with your work, Mr Constantine. I'm sure you're a very busy man.' He started towards the door and waited until he had his hand on the knob before he turned back. 'Thank you for talking to me. You've been a great help. More than you could possibly imagine.' As he opened the door he wanted to add 'I'll be back,' but he managed to restrain himself. He hoped that telling Constantine he had been helpful had worried the man a little bit, because that was the biggest lie of all.

7

Cass woke early, but Hector had already left. The range had been stoked up and a pot of coffee was keeping warm on top. She had barely poured her first cup when the phone rang. Liz sounded breathless.

'Hi, Cass. I've only got a minute. I'll swear everyone and their dog has fallen over in Norton this morning. A and E is jumping. I just wanted to let you know Mrs Shelton is awake and talking. The police are on their way, but they won't stay long. If you get over here in about an hour and ask for me, I'll see if I can get you in to see her.'

'Thanks, Liz.'

Cass took her time finishing her toast and several mugs of coffee, then went outside to clear her car of snow. This time she used conventional methods, an ice scraper and a soft brush, and her dear little Mini started on the first try. The main roads were clear, but piles of dirty slush lay in the gutters. She managed to find a parking space in the hospital car park and went inside to ask for Liz at the reception desk. Her friend arrived within minutes.

'Your boyfriend caused quite a stir this morning. He upset Mrs Shelton and made her cry. The registrar said he won't let her have any more visitors, but I'll ask her if she'll see you. I may have to sneak you in, so get yourself a coffee while I try to sort it out.'

'I need to speak to her, Liz. She may know where my mother is.'

Cass didn't want another coffee — she was already high on caffeine already — but she needed something to do with her hands. She wondered how Noel had managed to upset Mary. It wasn't like him to make a woman cry, but she knew how much he wanted to find Dora. Maybe he was getting desperate enough to feel harsh measures were called for. She could only hope Mary would agree to see her.

Liz came back at a run. Her spiky hair was in more of a mess than usual and she looked hot and tired. But even in her unflattering nurse's uniform, she still managed to look like a rock star. 'Mrs Shelton said no at first, but when I told her how worried you were about your mother, she changed her mind. The reg has gone for a coffee break, so by the time you get up to the ward you'll have about ten minutes to talk to her. She's in a side room on her own — room number eleven on the second floor — but I didn't tell you that. Just get out of there as soon as you can, and if anyone asks, you haven't seen me at all today.'

'Thanks, Liz,' Cass said gratefully. 'I'll speak to you tonight.' She hurried to the lift, hoping Mary Shelton hadn't changed her mind by the time she found the right room. She silently cursed Noel. Surely the man had conducted enough interviews with nervous and injured patients to know how to avoid upsetting a fragile old lady.

She followed the numbers to Mary's room and then hesitated. The door wasn't shut and she could only see part of a bed and a chair. She moved closer and peered through the gap. No one else was in the room as far as she could see. Mary looked up as soon as Cass entered the room. She was a small woman, and looked even smaller in the high hospital bed. Her face was bruised, but she had a look in her eyes that said she was still well enough to take care of herself. Cass had a feeling it wouldn't pay to beat about the bush, and besides, she didn't have the time.

She should have brought something, she thought. Only a fool visits someone in hospital without a gift of some sort, particularly if you want information from that person, but it was too late now. She moved across the room towards the bed a little tentatively, not sure of her reception.

'Hello, dear,' Mary said. 'Come and

sit beside me.' She waved in the direction of the single plastic chair. 'Have you heard anything about your mother? I've been so worried about her.'

Cass apologised for her lack of flowers and then shook her head. 'No one has heard anything from Dora. That's why I needed to speak to you, Mary. What happened to her?'

'I don't know. If I did, I promise I'd tell you. I feel so guilty for asking her to come and see me. That man, that policeman who asked me all those questions, he thought it was Bradley who took her, but it wasn't.'

'Bradley's gone missing, Mary, and someone saw a car outside your house the day you got hurt.'

'It wasn't Bradley's car. I don't care what the policeman says; it wasn't Bradley who came to the house. He wouldn't do that to me. It was a big man, much bigger than Bradley. He told me he wanted the ring, the emerald my father brought back from

138

abroad. I didn't want him to have it, so I pretended to look for it, but when I said I couldn't find it he pushed me down the stairs.' She coughed to clear her throat and Cass handed her the glass of water on the bedside table.

'The ring is quite safe, Mary. The police have it now. It was in my mother's handbag. I can understand it having a sentimental value, especially if it belonged to your father, but it wouldn't fetch more than a few hundred pounds if anyone tried to sell it. The emerald is quite nice, but I'm not even sure the setting is gold. It might have some rarity value I suppose, but it doesn't seem worth someone going to all that trouble.'

Mary sighed. 'People kill for a mobile phone, Cassandra. That ring might not be worth much, but if Bradley talked about it to someone and said it was set with a real emerald, they might have thought it was worth thousands.'

'That's possible, I suppose.' Cass leaned forward and took Mary's hand.

'You would tell me if it was Bradley who hurt you, wouldn't you? The inspector needs to know so they don't waste time looking in the wrong place for my mother. I need to find her soon because she may be hurt as well.'

'No, it wasn't Bradley. I haven't seen my son for weeks. He used to visit his grandma in her old cottage quite often when she was alive — he thought the world of her — but he knows I won't give him any more money to gamble away, so he doesn't come round very often.' She was silent for a moment and Cass glanced at her watch; she didn't have much time left. 'The man who pushed me,' Mary continued, 'probably knows Bradley, because he had that same mark on his hand. Bradley belongs to a club and they stamp your hand when you join. I think it's called the Bat Club. You should talk to the owner.'

Cass shuddered. She wouldn't go near that place again if someone paid her. Once was quite enough. In

140

future, she would leave Noel to sort out the enigmatic Lucien Constantine. She knew he wasn't really the devil, but he had done a damn good impersonation.

'Why did you give the emerald ring to Dora?' she asked as she got up from her uncomfortable seat. 'Did you want me to do something with it for you? Make it smaller, maybe?'

Mary looked sheepish. 'I really wanted you to value it for me, but you've already done that. I don't think it will pay off my mortgage, like I hoped, but it might buy me a few days' holiday when I get out of here.'

'I'm not able to give you a proper valuation, Mary. I know stones, but I would still be guessing. The setting looks old. Do you know how your father came by it?'

At that moment the door burst open and a woman in a dark blue dress stormed into the room. 'Mrs Shelton is not allowed visitors. The doctor has given strict orders. I don't know who let you in, but you'll have to leave right now.'

'I asked her to come,' Mary said quickly. 'She's only been here a few minutes and she's about to go. She's my friend's daughter and I wanted to see her.'

'All the same . . . '

Cass held up her hand. 'I'm going right this minute. Nice to see you, Mary. Get well soon.' She slunk out of the door as if she had been given a dressing-down by the headmistress. Had she managed to get any more information than Noel? She had no idea, but a visit to the police station seemed in order. Perhaps if they put their heads together . . . No, definitely not a good idea. The ever-present electrical sparks would probably blow their brains out.

She was just getting into her car when her phone rang. 'Where are you?' Noel asked her.

She didn't answer. It was her policy not to answer any question asked in that tone of voice.

'Cass? Are you there?'

Where is 'there'? she wondered. If he knew where she was, he didn't need to ask, and she was sure he knew exactly where she was. 'At the hospital.'

'I presume you tried to see Mary Shelton. I could have saved you a trip. The doctor won't let her see anyone.'

'Except me.'

He was quiet for so long it made her smile. 'You got in to see her?' he asked at last. 'Mary Shelton?'

'Yes,' she answered smugly, 'Mary Shelton. We had a nice little chat about ten minutes ago.'

'Meet me at the coffee shop. The one in the square. Five minutes.'

Noel Raven was still giving her orders and she almost decided not to turn up, but she wanted to tell him what she knew, and she was hungry. This was going to cost him more than just a coffee.

With a chicken and mayo sandwich on her plate, complete with a portion of fries, she was almost ready to forgive him. Some people just have an unfortunate manner, her grandmother used to say, and Noel was obviously one of them. But the café was crowded and he had managed to get a table.

'Did she admit her son pushed her down the stairs?' he began. 'Does she know where he is? What did she tell you?'

Cass held up her hand. She had her mouth full and he was going to have to wait. Eventually she said, 'Lots of stuff she didn't tell you, obviously. As a matter of fact, she was delighted to see me.'

He leaned across the table until his face was only inches from hers. 'Tell me what you know, Cassandra, right this minute, or I will put you over my knee and spank you in front of everyone.'

The images that flashed in front of her eyes made her toes curl. She ignored the tingle of electricity that coursed through her body. 'Is that a promise?' she asked wickedly.

He leaned back in his chair, a dimple forming at the side of his mouth as he smiled at her. 'Not here, and not now, but definitely later. And if you don't tell me everything I want to know, I can think of other forms of punishment.'

'Goodness me,' she said, fluttering her eyelashes at him. 'You are such a brutal interrogator. How can I refuse?'

'Finish your sandwich while I get you a coffee.' He got to his feet. 'And then you can tell me everything Mary told you.' He paused with his hand on the back of her chair. 'We need to get Dora back, Cass.'

His words took the smile off her face like he knew they would, but he was a policeman and he was just doing his job. The trouble was, she wanted more from him, but she wasn't prepared to give any more of herself, so it always finished up as a stalemate. Perhaps it always would. 'So Mary Shelton told you it wasn't her son who ransacked her house,' he said. 'It was some other man with the same tattoo. Bradley is the obvious suspect, Cass. Are you sure you believe her?'

She nodded. 'Yes, I do. She's worried about Dora. She thinks it was all her fault for inviting my mother to her house in the first place.'

'I think your mother probably saved her life by calling the police station. The ambulance was there within minutes.'

Cass finished her sandwich and picked up her coffee. 'That man I saw in here the other morning — he was big, and he had that tattoo on his wrist.'

'That would be a bit of a coincidence, wouldn't it?'

'Not really. Not if he lives on this side of town. This is the only coffee shop around here, and the only one that serves halfway decent coffee. That's why it's always so crowded.'

'Doesn't help, though, does it? We either have to put a twenty-four-hour watch on the place, or hope we bump into him by accident. Besides, there are probably a lot of big men around here with a bat tattoo.'

Cass raised an eyebrow. 'You think?'

Noel sighed. He looked tired. She knew he was as worried about Dora as she was. 'I went to the Bat Club, Cass. I saw Constantine. He told me he has Bradley Shelton staying with him.'

Cass blinked. 'Staying with him? What does that mean? Is Bradley staying willingly, or is he a prisoner?'

'I don't know. Constantine wouldn't tell me anything else. He could very well be lying, or he could just as easily have Bradley locked up somewhere.' She began to speak but he raised a hand to stop her. 'The most worrying thing is that if Constantine has Bradley, who has your mother?'

'The big man with the bat tattoo.'

'That's one possibility. The other is that Bradley took her somewhere, possibly locked her up, and then got picked up by Constantine.'

'In which case my mother may be locked up somewhere, possibly without food or water. You have to talk to Bradley, Noel. Raid the Bat Club or something. I bet Constantine has drugs there. You could arrest him.'

'No I couldn't. There is nothing to show Constantine has done anything wrong. I can't just barge in and arrest him for nothing. He'd laugh in my face.'

She pushed her chair back and stood up. 'If you won't do it, I'll go and see Lucien Constantine again myself. I'll make him tell me where my mother is.'

'And then I'll have to come looking for you, instead of trying to find Dora. You know if you go back to the club he'll find some way of keeping you there. He enjoyed winding me up, and I bet he can't wait to do it again. You won't be helping, Cass. You'd be putting your mother in more danger than she's in already.'

Cass dropped back into her chair. She felt defeated. 'So what do we do next?' She could feel tears very close and swallowed hard. 'I don't know what to do, Noel.'

He reached across the table to put a

sympathetic hand over hers. She glanced down and then jumped back in alarm. The emerald ring gleamed on his finger, sending little flecks of light dancing on the coffee shop ceiling.

'Why on earth are you wearing that? You said you were going to put it in the police safe.'

'I did, but after I spoke to Constantine I thought I'd get it out and have another look at it.'

She looked at him in horror. 'You didn't have to put it on. What if you can't get it off this time?'

'Then I'll have to wear it forever.' He tried to take her hand again but she pulled it away. 'It's no big deal, Cass.'

'Yes, I think it is.' She lowered her voice to a whisper, glancing round the café to make sure no one was listening. 'It's not an ordinary ring, Noel. I knew that when I first saw it. It's like my sapphire, the one my father gave to me.'

He held up his hand and stared at the ring with new interest. 'You think this ring is magic?'

She looked round the room again. Even if no one was listening, someone might be watching them. 'No, of course not. I just think the ring is . . . you know, a bit special.'

He was grinning at her now. 'I'm wearing a magic ring. Wow!'

She wanted to hit him, and then wished she had hit him when she felt a tear run down her cheek. Whatever was wrong with her? She brushed at the offending wet steak with the back of her hand and saw his expression change.

'Are you crying? I'm so sorry, darling. What's wrong?'

She looked at him is frustration. How could he possibly not know? 'I'm just tired of it all, Noel. I want to find my mother. She's been gone almost three days now, and everything seems to point to that awful man at the club. But you're telling me you can't do anything about him.' Another tear followed the first and she slapped at it angrily. 'I have no idea where Hector is or what he's doing, and Tobias misses Dora so much he just prowls around the house meowing. The poor animal is probably trying to tell me something, but I can't speak cat. I need to do something to help my mother, but I don't know what.' She could hear the petulant whine in her voice and hated it. She sounded like a small child crying for her missing parent.

'I've got some of my men doing a search of the area, but whoever took Dora away took her in a car, so she could be anywhere by now. If it was Bradley who took her, I think she'll be somewhere fairly close by; but if it was someone else, then I just don't know where to start.'

Cass suddenly remembered something. 'Bradley's gran lived close by. Not far out of town. Mary said he used to visit his grandma a lot when she was alive. She had trouble getting around, so he probably has a key. Do you think the house might still be empty?'

Noel got up and slipped on his jacket. 'I have no idea, but it's somewhere to start. Go home, Cass, and get some rest. I'll let you know if I find anything.'

'I'm too worried about my mother to rest. You always tell me the first twenty-four hours are crucial, and Dora's been missing for three days.' She pulled on her own coat, shrugging into it before Noel could help her. 'So I'm not going home. I'm coming with you.'

'I'll have to go back to the station to find out where the house is, and if Constantine is lying and Bradley is still there, it could be dangerous.'

'I don't care,' Cass said stubbornly. 'I'm still coming with you.'

8

It took Noel all of ten minutes on the computer to find the address of the house where old Mrs Shelton had lived. It was a farm cottage in the middle of a field, by the look of the map. There were no house numbers, so Noel's satnav would be useless. And it was snowing again.

The roads through the town centre were clear of snow, but once he and Cass got out into the country things got trickier, with the car sliding on icy patches and bumping over drifts. 'Wet snow on top of ice,' he said. 'Not a good combination.'

Cass wished they had brought her car instead of Noel's low-slung sports car. She could hear a grating noise every time they went over a frozen mound of snow, and she was sure that any minute they were going to get stuck. The thought of being stuck in the middle this white wilderness scared her a lot, and she worried even more about her mother. Was there any possibility that the little witch was really still alive?

From a distance the two isolated farm cottages looked like humps in the white landscape, with no definition to turn them into houses. But as they got nearer Cass could see how rundown they both were. The gate was hanging off the picket fence in front of one, and the other didn't have a gate at all. 'Which one?' she asked.

Noel brought the car to a stop. 'The one with the car outside, I would imagine. The other one looks derelict.'

Cass sat up in her seat. 'You think Bradley's still here?'

'I don't know, but that's not Bradley Shelton's car. Not the one registered in his name, anyway.' He undid his seatbelt. 'Stay in the car, Cass. I'll go the rest of the way on foot.'

'Oh, don't be so ridiculous,' she said impatiently. 'You'll fall into a snowdrift or something. Besides, if he sees you coming, he'll jump into his car and get away. Why don't you drive right up to the door and block him in?'

Noel gave her a dirty look. He didn't like being given orders, either, but he started the engine again and drove nearer to the house.

They were both waiting for someone to appear, but when nothing happened Noel got out, holding up his hand to tell Cass to stay where she was. She let him go, but then moved across to the driver's side so she could keep the engine running in case they needed to make a quick getaway. She had believed Mary when the woman had said her son wasn't involved; but if Bradley wasn't in the house, then who was it? She hoped with all her heart it wasn't Lucien Constantine. He scared her more than anyone she had ever met. But from what she had seen of the man, he wasn't likely to do his own dirty work. He had people to do that for him.

Noel had disappeared round the side

of the house, presumably to try the back door, but now everything had gone quiet. Cass opened her door and heard a bird chirping in a snow-covered tree.

It was much too quiet. Maybe Noel had found her mother's body and was afraid to come out and tell her. She left the car engine running while she hurried down the slippery path to the cottage. She almost knocked on the front door, but then realised that might be a bit stupid. So might peering through the front window. Instead, she hunkered down and crept round the side of the house, following Noel's footprints in the snow.

When she got round the back she could hear voices inside the house. Not raised or angry, just normal conversational tones. It would be just like Noel to leave her out in the cold while he had tea and biscuits with someone inside.

She pushed open the kitchen door and came face to face with her father.

'Good afternoon, Cassandra.'

Cass looked from one to the other of the two men. Her father was the last person she had expected to see. 'I left the car engine running,' she said inanely. 'Shall I go and turn it off?'

Noel shook his head. 'No, we're just leaving. We know Dora isn't here, because Hector has made a thorough search of the rooms, but she has been here. She wrote a message on a biscuit wrapper.' He handed Cass the torn piece of paper.

Thursday morning. Going to try and find the farmhouse. I can keep myself warm for a while, so don't worry about me.

'It's Friday today,' Cass said with a catch in her voice. The two men looked at one another.

'I'm positive she's still alive,' Hector said. 'It really depends how far she managed to get. If she was weak from lack of food and water, she might not be able to keep heating her body with the warming spell. It would take a lot of energy to keep a spell like that going for

157

any length of time.'

'So where's the main farm house?' Cass asked.

'That's the problem,' Noel said. 'It was pulled down some years ago when the farm was no longer profitable.'

'But we can still look for her, can't we? If Dora left here she must be somewhere.' Like wandering about in the snowy fields trying to keep herself warm, Cass thought. She remembered the bright pashmina. At least that should stand out against a white background.

Hector held open the front door. 'We'll take my off-roader and leave your car here, Noel. No sense in getting stuck in a drift. I got the car rental company to give me something sensible when I landed at Stansted and saw what the English weather was like.'

Hector always parked his car in the barn behind the house; that was why Cass hadn't recognised it. She wondered where he'd been. Abroad, obviously, but she had no idea where or what for. 'I know you work for a government department,' she said as she climbed into the back of the big car. 'But what exactly do you do?'

'Long story, Cassandra.' He looked over his shoulder to make sure her seatbelt was fastened properly. 'Let's just say my job is to keep things in proportion. Magic has a place in the modern world, but it can't be allowed to take over and cause harm. I'm much like Noel, really — just a policeman.'

'I thought you chased spies,' she said as he pulled away from the cottage.

'If I told people I monitor the perpetrators of dark magic, I doubt they would believe me.'

'Sounds good, though,' Noel said. 'Much better than just a policeman.'

Cass was staring out through the windscreen, hoping to see a flash of mauve. 'Do you have a plan?' she asked. 'Or are we going to drive round in circles? It'll be dark in an hour.'

'I'm heading for the place where the farmhouse used to be,' Hector told her.

'I thought I saw a building through the trees.'

The building turned out to be a modern house set in snow-covered gardens. A light was on in a downstairs window. Hector brought the car to a standstill and turned round in his seat. 'Someone's at home.'

Cass felt her heart start to race. The house was about a mile from the cottages, a difficult trek in these conditions, but she knew her mother was stronger than she looked. There was a toughness about the little woman that didn't show on the surface.

The three of them were standing in the snow, looking at the house, when the front door opened. Dora smiled at them. She looked in far better condition than her rescuers. Cass gave a little squeal and rushed to hug her mother. Hector wasn't far behind, and Noel had a big smile on his face. Cass found she had tears running down her face and brushed them away quickly.

Dora held the door open and they all

moved into the warmth of the house. 'The owners are obviously away somewhere,' she said, 'but all the services are still connected and the fridge is fully stocked. I've kept a tally of what I've eaten so it can be replaced.' She looked at Hector reproachfully. 'I've been here almost forty-eight hours. What took you so long?'

He laughed. 'I knew you were safe somewhere. It was just a matter of tracking you down.'

'I'll make us all tea,' Dora said, 'and then I'll tell you exactly what happened to me. Do you have your notebook with you, Noel?'

He reached into his pocket and pulled out a small spiral-bound one. 'It's a good job I'm prepared for all contingencies,' he said with a grin.

'The landline is down because of all the snow. That's why I couldn't contact anyone. I thought of using another bird.' Dora smiled at Noel. 'But I knew one of you would find me in the end.' She looked around the comfortable, well-furnished room. 'And this place is much nicer than the farm cottage.'

'We went there first,' Cass told her mother. 'I've been so worried about you. Did Mary's son kidnap you and take you to the cottage?'

Hector silenced her with a look. 'Let you mother do this her own way, Cassandra. Tea always comes first.'

Once they were all seated, with a large tray of tea and biscuits in front of them, Dora started at the beginning with her visit to Mary Shelton's house. 'I don't know if it was Bradley,' she said. 'I've never met Mary's son, so I don't know what he looks like.'

Noel produced the photo of Bradley he had been carrying around with him and Dora shook her head dismissively. 'No, it wasn't him. The man who grabbed me was big and tall. He held a knife to my throat.' She looked up at Hector. 'You'll have to teach me how to turn a bad person into a frog. I could have got the bus home and saved all this running around.' She took a sip of her tea. 'But whoever he was, he was looking for the emerald ring I had in my handbag. Did you find it?'

Noel held up his hand where the emerald gleamed on his ring finger. 'I've already explained to Hector why I'm wearing this. He thinks it has some magical powers, and maybe it was Lucien Constantine who instigated the search at Mary Shelton's house.' He smiled at Cass sheepishly. 'You were quite right. Now I've put it on, I can't get it off. Believe me, I've tried. A whole bowlful of oil wouldn't shift it.'

Cass looked down at the ring on her right hand, where the star sapphire pulsed in time with her heartbeat, and wondered what would happen if the two rings were in contact with one another. A half-remembered phrase had been haunting her: *Together we are invincible*.

'Lucien Constantine,' Dora said. 'I've met him, haven't I? I didn't like the man. I've seen evil before, and I've discovered it comes in many forms

— most of them human.'

'Why would Lucien want the emerald?' Noel asked. 'Cass said it isn't worth that much. Not the price of GBH, burglary and abduction.'

'Power,' Hector answered. 'The ring will give the wearer power, and Lucien is all about power. Power is what motivates him.' He looked at Noel. 'I think Lucien Constantine would be quite prepared to kill for that ring.'

'Thanks a bundle,' Noel said dryly. 'It worries me a bit that I can't get the damned thing off my finger. Do you think Constantine would go so far as to cut off my finger just to get the ring?'

'I'm sure he would. I suggest you find out how to use those powers before you lose your digit.'

Dora put down her empty cup and picked up the tray. 'The Fab Four,' she said. 'Isn't that what those superheroes were called? We must surely have enough power between us to face up to Constantine and defeat him.'

Hector took the tray from his wife.

'Wars are bloody, Pandora, and there are often casualties. It would be safer to use our wits.'

Cass was sure everyone's wits must have completely deserted them. Her mother was actually talking about a gang of superheroes, and her father seriously thought Noel could lose his finger. Had they all gone completely mad? She knew gemstones could generate power. A crystal had been used in the first radio set. But not magical power. Everything had a logical explanation; you just had to find it. She still couldn't get her head round the idea of real magic.

They were all silent for a few minutes while Dora put the cups in the dishwasher. 'Should we leave the owners a note or something to say we've been here?'

Noel shrugged. 'You can if you want, but I'll contact them as soon as I get back and let them know their house was instrumental in saving a woman's life.'

'They might want to know how I got in.'

'How *did* you get in?' he asked curiously.

'Magic again, I expect.' Cass picked up her coat and shrugged into it. It still felt damp and she wasn't looking forward to putting on her boots; she could see them steaming. She saw her mother and father smile at one another, and wondered how her mother could accept Hector coming and going the way he did. He behaved more like a lodger than a husband, but perhaps that was why their marriage worked.

Hector took them to Noel's car, which was still parked outside the cottage, and then they drove in convoy back to Abracadabra. Cass could see her mother relax once they got home. Noel was invited to stay for dinner, but declined because he had work to do. Cass sank gratefully into a chair. The kitchen was warm and fuggy and she thought she might go to sleep if she sat for too long. Hector stoked the fire while Dora put a loaf of bread in the oven to warm. It all seemed so normal that Cass found it difficult to believe her mother was a witch and her father a warlock, a man who chased demons for a living.

She got to her feet and made her mother sit down. 'I'm going to pour you a glass of wine and then I'll finish preparing the food. For goodness sake, Mother, just sit down for five minutes. You must be exhausted.'

'I've been sitting down for the last twenty-four hours. There was nothing to do in that house except watch TV.' She patted Cass's hand. 'They had a lovely bathroom with a Jacuzzi bathtub, so I had a nice soak last night.'

Cass knew her mother was making light of her ordeal. It must have been terrifying to be held at knifepoint by a strange man, and then abducted and kept in a cold farm cottage. She wondered how her mother had managed the long walk through the snow to the house, but she didn't ask. It was bound to involve magic of some sort.

Dinner was a pot of Dora's home-made vegetable soup with warm bread and a big dish of homemade butter, the red wine a perfect accompaniment.

'We need to talk,' Hector said. 'But we need sleep more than conversation, so we'll reconvene in the morning; and if Noel can get away for a couple of hours, all the better. We have to sort out a strategy.'

Cass stared at him blankly. A strategy? What did he think they were, a battalion of the armed forces? 'We have Dora back. Isn't that what we set out to do in the first place? What more needs doing?'

Hector seemed to be weighing up his words before he spoke. 'Constantine wants the ring, and Noel has the ring. I think Noel would happily hand the emerald over without an argument, but for one thing it doesn't belong to him, and for another he can't get it off his finger.'

'He can have it cut off,' Cass said. 'It

won't be a problem. I have the tools to do it right here, and I can make the ring almost as good as new afterwards.'

Hector studied her for a moment, his face serious. 'I don't think that will work, Cassandra, but by all means try. We'll get Noel to come to your studio tomorrow.' He put his hand on her shoulder. 'Get to bed now, daughter. I'll take care of your mother.'

He hadn't told her why trying to cut Noel's ring off wouldn't work, and she hadn't asked, as she didn't really want to know the answer. She was too tired to cope with witchcraft and wizardry; just wanted to crawl into bed and go to sleep. Her mother was safe, and that was all she cared about. Hector probably wanted some time alone with his wife, and she was quite happy for them to talk about supernatural goings-on all night as long as she wasn't in the room. The thought that Noel might be in danger did worry her, but she was sure she could get the ring off his finger in the morning, as long as it wasn't some strange metal she knew nothing about. That thought stayed with her as she slid into sleep. She dreamed of Lucien Constantine chasing Noel round a warehouse filled with enormous saws while she tried to find his missing finger.

Cass awoke in a bedroom filled with moonlight and shadows and heard someone moving about downstairs. Not of a particularly nervous disposition, even after a bad dream, she decided it must be her father or her mother and went to investigate. The house was still pleasantly warm, but she pulled on a dressing gown and slippers. You never knew who or what you might meet in the middle of the night in a house called Abracadabra.

Hector greeted her with a smile when she walked into the kitchen. 'Warm milk,' he said, holding up a mug, 'and a pinch of your mother's sleeping potion. You have this one, and I'll make myself another. I dropped some of the potion in your mother's drink before she went to bed, so she should be out cold until the morning.'

Cass smiled as she took the proffered mug. 'Dosing her with her own medicine is poetic justice, isn't it? She's always doing it to me.'

'Did something wake you? Not me, I hope.'

She sat beside him on the sofa. 'A bad dream woke me. I dreamed Lucien had cut off Noel's finger. Not a portent of things to come, I hope.'

'I'll do my best to make sure no harm comes to Noel, Cassandra. You two are both halves of a whole. You need one another.'

Cass frowned. 'I don't want to need anyone. I'm fine on my own, thank you. Besides, Noel has no intention of settling down. He told me relationships scare him.'

'They scare me, too,' Hector said with a smile. 'But whatever we may think, we can't do without them. You can try and change your destiny, Cassandra, but that will only lead to pain and sorrow.'

So might a life with Noel Raven, she thought, but sometimes it was fun to live dangerously.

9

Cass dragged herself out of bed the next morning at seven, even though her body was screaming for more sleep. She had done very little the day before except sit in a car, but she felt as if she had climbed a mountain. Her whole body ached and she felt as if she had a bout of flu coming on. If Dora had a magic potion in her cupboard, now was the time to swallow her pride and ask for help.

The kitchen was already occupied by her father and mother, who were sitting at the kitchen table doing a crossword. Cass thought if she had to face much more domestic bliss she might throw up. It was just too sickly-sweet this early in the morning.

Dora greeted Cass with a big smile, but one look at her daughter's face turned the smile into a frown. 'How much did you give her?' she asked Hector.

He shrugged. 'A few drops. The same dose I took myself.'

Dora got up from the table. 'You should have halved the amount for Cass. Our bodies will only use the exact amount we need for a good night's sleep, but Cassie can't control her metabolism like we can. You drugged her.' She was already pulling out bottles and looking at labels. 'This should do the trick.' She poured a thick yellow liquid into a spoon and held it out.

Cass pulled a face and turned her head away. The stuff smelled of orange peel and garlic. For one moment she thought her mother might hold her nose until she opened her mouth, a manoeuvre she could remember from her childhood, but Dora just waited patiently until Cass reluctantly took the spoon and swallowed the yellow gloop.

'It will make you feel better, dear.'

Cass had heard those words before as

well, but the stuff worked almost instantly. She was glad it was only an overdose of her mother's sleeping potion that had made her feel so weak, and not some awful virus. Five minutes later she was ready for her father's scrambled eggs and her mother's hot buttered toast. Actually, she decided, they did make quite a good team. Particularly in the kitchen. Coffee followed, and by then Noel had turned up on the doorstep.

'I have to be back by 10.30,' he said. 'I have another interview with Mrs Shelton at her home.'

Dora handed him a cup of coffee. 'If Mary's out of hospital, I must go and visit her. Would you like me to come with you, Noel? She might be more inclined to talk if I'm there as well.'

He nodded and took the slice of toast Hector handed to him. 'Great idea, Dora. For some reason the woman took an instant dislike to me.'

'Not hard to do,' Cass said brightly, 'but I'm sure she'll get over it.'

'That's not hard to do, either. You didn't like me at first, but now you love me to bits, don't you, darling?'

'See, Hector?' Dora said, exasperation tinging her voice. 'They behave like a couple of children most of the time. They both need to grow up.'

'We're not related, are we?' Noel asked with feigned horror. 'That would really mess up my future plans.'

'If you were my brother,' Cass hissed at him, 'you wouldn't be sitting here now. I'd have killed you long ago.'

Hector held up his hand. 'May I remind you, this is a strategy meeting. We need to clear the table and get on with it. We don't have much time.'

'Noel wants me to try to get the ring off his finger,' Cass reminded her father. 'It should only take a few minutes.'

'Then I suggest we all adjourn to your studio, Cassandra. But I'm afraid this could be more difficult than you think — possibly even dangerous. If this ring is an ancient talisman, it'll choose the wearer and then become part of him.'

So the only way to get rid of it would be amputation. She could manage that as well, if necessary. Cass pushed her hair out of her eyes and headed for her studio, the other three following behind. She had a special ring saw that had a little protective hook to fit between the finger and the saw. Or she could use a tried-and-tested method of wrapping the finger tightly and slipping a piece of the material under the ring before unwinding it. The ring definitely wasn't made of titanium, and as far as she knew, that was the only metal impossible to saw through.

She was happy with the state of Noel's finger because it wasn't swollen at all, but when she greased his finger and tried to twist the ring, it didn't move. And it definitely should have done. 'Normally, if I push really hard on the underside of the ring I can slip the protective piece of the saw between the ring and the finger,' she explained. She peered at his finger through her loupe, then looked up at Hector worriedly. 'But this time the ring seems to be attached to the skin somehow, as if it grew there.'

'Embedded,' Hector said. 'That's the word you want. The ring has chosen its owner and become embedded.'

'So where does that leave me?' Noel asked. 'I don't want to wear a ring. Actually, I don't like jewellery of any sort. Even my watch is nothing fancy; it just tells the time.' He waved his hand in the air. 'I want the ring off.'

'Then you shouldn't have put it on,' Cass said impatiently. She had told him to leave it in the safe, but no, he had to take it out and put the damned thing on his finger again. 'I can't do anything for you, so you'll have to go to the hospital and see what they can do.'

Dora had come over to stand beside her husband. 'They won't be able to get it off, either,' she said. 'Not without amputation, and I thought we were trying to avoid that. Besides, when they see what's happened they'll ask all sorts of difficult questions, and then Constantine will know exactly where to look for the artefact he wants so badly.'

'Did you get a good look at the ring when you took it off Noel's finger the first time?' Hector asked.

Cass nodded. 'Yes, I examined it thoroughly. There are some quite large inclusions in the emerald, which is why I told Mary it wasn't very valuable; but now that I've looked again, I think they're meant to be there. They're too uniform to be natural. And I still haven't worked out what the metal is. It looks like gold, but I have no idea what sort of gold.' She thought for a moment. 'There was some sort of inscription on the inside of the band, and some little indentations too evenly spaced to be random. I took a photo because the writing looked similar to the carvings on the ring you gave me for my birthday.' She handed Hector her phone. 'See if you can work out what they mean.'

He studied the picture on her screen, spreading his fingers to make it bigger. 'I've never seen anything like this before, but there are lots of things on this earth I've never seen before.'

'It might be less painful to settle for amputation.' Noel said. 'Let's face it, if Constantine catches up with me, he won't be gentle. He'll just pull my finger off.'

Dora patted his hand. 'Lucien can't harm you, Noel. I'm sure the ring is capable of stopping that evil man before he gets anywhere near you.'

'Like surrounding him with a force-field, or something?' Cass put her saw back in the drawer. 'You've all been watching too much TV. The writing on the inside of the ring is probably a maker's name in a foreign language, and the ring is stuck because Noel's finger is swollen. He'll just have to wait for the swelling to go down.'

'Or work out what powers the ring actually possesses, if any.' Noel rubbed his hand. 'Cass, you know stones. What magical powers does an emerald have?'

She wanted to tell him gemstones didn't have special powers, but she knew that wasn't true, and Noel wanted some sort of reassurance. She had to admit that the idea of losing a finger wasn't pleasant, whatever method was used.

'An emerald is supposed to have a calming effect. It also opens up the mind to things unseen by the naked eye. The supernatural, maybe. Some people say it gives the wearer the ability to see the future. It is also the stone of eternal love and should be worn on the ring finger.' She looked at Noel. 'That's why I asked you why you put it on that particular finger.'

'When I first tried it on, it was the only finger it fitted properly.' He looked down at his hand. 'But it hasn't had much of a calming effect.'

Cass smiled at him. 'I think it has. If I thought Constantine was coming to tear my finger off, I'd be frightened to death.'

He grinned at her. 'Actually I am frightened death, but I like to keep up the macho image if I possibly can.'

'Which brings us full circle,' Hector said. 'What are we going to do about Constantine?'

Cass led the way back to the kitchen. 'Noel can't arrest him, because he has all the paperwork he needs to run that club legitimately.'

'I can't get a search warrant, either,' Noel said, 'without any evidence of wrongdoing, which is a shame because I'm sure we'd find drugs.' He sat down at the kitchen table and the others joined him. Tobias looked up sleepily, wondering whether any food was likely to be forthcoming.

Dora filled the kettle at the sink and turned it on, then sat down and looked across the table at her husband. 'Why don't you tell us what you really do, Hector? I think Cassie deserves to be told what her father does for a living.'

Cass frowned at her mother. Was something new about to be thrown into the pot? She didn't like surprises. 'You told us you worked for some obscure government department making sure magic doesn't get out of hand,' she said. 'What does that have to do with Lucien Constantine and the emerald ring? You said he can't do magic.'

Hector sighed. 'Just about everything, as it happens.' He waited while Dora filled mugs with tea and handed them round. 'There has always been black magic as well as white magic, but if the balance of power is kept fairly even, then everything jogs along quite well. Constantine is trying to shift that balance by hunting down all the magic artefacts. That's why he wants the emerald ring.'

'And is evidently prepared to tear my finger off to get it.' Noel rubbed his hand again. 'It's a good job I wasn't wearing it when I visited him at the club.'

'He doesn't know you've got it,' Cass

183

said. 'Not yet, anyway. He didn't mention it when I was there. He noticed my sapphire, but he seemed . . . not scared, exactly, just wary of it. Would it have kept me safe from him, Hector?'

'I don't know. I hope so — that's why I gave it to you — but I wouldn't advise you to put it to the test.'

She shuddered. 'I don't intend to.'

'What will Constantine do next?' Dora asked.

'That's difficult to answer.' Hector rubbed a hand over his face. 'At the moment he has no idea Noel has the ring. He may think it's at the police station, but he can't get to it there, or not very easily. We may have to give him a clue, or perhaps use a little bait.'

'Like sending me back to the club to wave my finger under his nose?' Noel said.

Hector gave Noel a thoughtful look. 'That might work.'

'Stop it! Both of you.' Cass felt sick thinking about it. 'It's not funny.'

Noel pulled a face. 'I don't think Hector meant it as a joke, Cass. I think he was deadly serious.'

She threw up her hands, knowing she looked like a child having a tantrum, but unable to stop herself. How could four adults sit round a table and discuss finger amputation and magic rings as if it were the most natural thing in the world? She craved normality, but deep in her heart she knew that wasn't going to happen. Perhaps she'd wake up one morning and find it was all a dream, but she didn't think that was going to happen either.

Noel was still rubbing his finger, and she remembered thinking the stupid man would never get the ring off if he kept doing that. She felt sick with worry for him. She had seen Constantine, and everything her father said about the man was true. He was pure evil. If he wanted the ring, he wouldn't give up until he had it. Cass wanted a normal life with normal parents, and tried to imagine sitting on a sofa in a modern house with two kids snuggled up beside her, perhaps a dog at her feet. When her husband walked through the front door, he looked a lot like Noel Raven. Her vision blurred, and she clutched the edge of the table for support, trying to stop herself sliding any further into nothingness.

Everyone had stopped talking and Hector grabbed her before she slid to the floor. Noel got to his feet, but he didn't move towards her. She could see the distress on his face as her father helped her back onto her chair.

'She was thinking about me,' Noel said. 'She does that when she thinks about me.'

Cass pushed Hector's arm away, forcing her mouth to function so she could speak. 'No, I don't. Not always. I wasn't thinking about you. I was just thinking about having kids.'

'Are you trying to say your thoughts about me weren't sexual? Then how did we manage to have kids in this vision of yours?'

She could feel herself blushing now, which was making her feel light-headed again. 'I didn't say they were yours.'

'How many did you have, for goodness sake? Were any of them mine?'

'Leave her alone, Noel.' Dora handed Cass a glass of water. 'It's ordinary water, Cassie. I haven't put anything in it. Just have a sip or two.'

'Hold his hand,' Hector said suddenly. 'Hold Noel's hand, Cassandra. I want to see what happens.'

She knew what her father meant. She knew exactly what he meant, because she had wondered the same thing herself. Confident her father wouldn't let any harm come to her, she stood up and held out her hand.

Noel didn't move. 'It's too dangerous.' He looked at Hector. 'If she passes out just thinking about me, what do you think will happen if I hold her hand?'

'Don't kid yourself, Noel,' Cass said. 'I don't like you very much right this moment, and I'm not having sexual thoughts about you, so I'm sure it will be fine.'

'Wait,' Dora said. 'This should be a proper scientific experiment, and we should prepare ourselves in case something does happen. Besides, Cassie needs a few moments to clear her head. Let me move the tea things before you start; I like my china and I don't want it broken because you all rushed into something you know nothing about.'

Cass didn't really believe her mother was more worried about her china than her daughter, but she could see the sense in not rushing into anything unprepared. She trusted her stones, and she was quite sure they wouldn't harm her; but when she glanced down at her ring and saw the star pulsing with extra brightness, she began to understand the need for caution.

Hector looked slightly put out, but he moved across the kitchen to help Dora.

'This is ridiculous,' Cass said. She had already let her outstretched hand fall to her side. 'If you have to go to all this trouble, let's not bother.'

Noel raised an eyebrow. 'Are you turning chicken, Cassandra Moon? Are you so afraid of holding my hand you're bottling out?'

She held out her right hand again and took a step toward him. 'I'm all for trying anything once. I held my hand out straight away, remember? You're the one who keeps saying it's too dangerous. So who's the chicken?'

She had expected to feel something when the rings touched — even a small show of sparks would have made it all worthwhile — but there was nothing. All she could feel was warmth; a warmth that moved through her body and comforted her. She looked down at her hand, snugly tucked inside his, and then lifted her head to smile at him.

'Anything?' Hector asked.

Noel shook his head. 'Nothing. That was a bit of a let-down, really, wasn't it?'

'So was I,' Cass said. She thought

about moving her hand, but it was comfortable where it was.

But it was Noel who dropped her hand, frowning at her. 'What did you say?'

'I agreed with you. I said I was expecting something more, as well.'

'I didn't say that.'

'Yes you did. I heard you.'

He stepped back. 'No, I didn't say it, Cass. I just thought it.'

She smiled pityingly at him. 'It won't work, Noel. The rings were in contact and nothing magical happened. Get used to the idea.'

Before she could stop him he took her hand again, but she snatched it back almost immediately. 'I am not a witch. You know I don't like being called that.'

Noel lifted both his hands, palms out. 'I rest my case.'

Cass was about to laugh at him. A joke can go on too long. But then she caught sight of her parents. Dora took as step forward, a resigned expression on her face, and Cass tried to speak, but her mouth was too dry to get her tongue round the words. Hector was finding it impossible to hide his excitement, and Noel just looked smug. He'd been proved right, and that was all he was thinking about at this precise moment. Probably. Cass knew if she held his hand again, she would be able to tell exactly what he was thinking.

10

Tobias got up and stretched, a low growl coming from deep in his throat. He jumped down from his chair and walked over to nudge Dora's legs. 'He's hungry,' she said, 'and so am I. Let's send out for pizza, and then we can discuss what just happened.'

Cass didn't want to discuss what had just happened. She wanted to forget all about it at the earliest possible moment. If they started talking about it, she might put her hands over her ears and sing 'la, la, la' until they stopped. It was stupid and childish, she knew, but she *felt* stupid and childish. She hated things she didn't understand.

Hector picked up the phone to call for food, and Cass got up from her chair and walked to the sofa where Noel was sitting. He looked a little shell-shocked, she thought, but he couldn't possibly feel as bad as she did.

'Sit down, Cass,' he said. 'I'm not going to hold your hand again, and unless I do, our thoughts are quite safe. Stop looking at me as if I'm staring into your soul. It was you who read my thoughts, remember, not the other way round.'

She sat beside him warily, not looking at him. 'Didn't you pick up any of mine when you were inside my head?'

'Not a single one, honestly. Perhaps it only works one way, a sender and receiver thing. But I have a feeling your father won't let us rest until he finds out exactly how it does work. We're going to be lab rats, and there's nothing we can do about it.'

She knew he was right, but she felt traumatised just thinking about it. What if Noel found out how she felt about him? If she tried to think about something else, she knew the thought she was trying to suppress would come popping to the surface. There would be no hiding it.

'We can't do this, Noel. You must have things you don't want anyone to know. We shouldn't have to share our innermost thoughts with anyone.'

'I don't believe that's going to happen. It would be like Babel — too much going on for anyone to comprehend. What exactly did you hear from me? Just those few words?'

She nodded. 'Yes, as if you'd said them aloud. But nothing else.'

'And in actual fact, there must have been a hundred things going through my head at that moment. I think this power may be selective and only pick up our main thought, the one on top at the time. So yes, it could be embarrassing, but I think it can be controlled.'

Cass was thinking it through now as well, and she didn't understand Hector's excitement. If the thought transference only happened between her and Noel, she couldn't see how it would help her father defeat Constantine.

The pizzas arrived in double-quick time, and Cass wondered if her mother used a delivery boy on a broomstick. Hector took a bottle of champagne out of the fridge and opened it with a pop. She watched him fill her glass, thinking this was probably a softening-up process, but that was fine by her. She could do with a drink, and maybe a dulling of the senses would help her deal with what was going to happen. She gave a surreptitious pull at her sapphire ring, but she knew it wouldn't move. Sometimes she could take it off without any trouble, but for some inexplicable reason she always put it on again. Right now it was stuck fast.

The pizza was delicious. Her mother had made coleslaw from something that looked like a traditional mixture of white cabbage and carrot, but probably wasn't. Cass was past caring, even though her father had deliberately restricted her intake of alcohol. She didn't want Noel to know how she felt about him, and she definitely didn't want to know how he felt about her. She was pretty sure it was more lust than love on his part, but while she didn't know for sure, she could let her imagination run wild now and again.

Get that thought out of your head right now, she told herself sternly as she watched her father move the champagne bottle out of her reach.

A strange sort of lethargy had settled over her, a 'whatever will be, will be' kind of mood, and Noel was looked as relaxed as she felt. The emerald gemstone was noted for its calming effect, and the sapphire had healing properties. With a bit of luck she'd go to sleep and wake up when it was all over, like having an anaesthetic at the dentist.

Once they had all finished eating, Hector started fidgeting, obviously anxious to start experimenting on them both; but Dora insisted on making coffee. And then Noel's phone started ringing.

'Sorry folks,' he said as he got to his feet, 'but there's a problem at the hospital. Mary has taken a turn for the worse and they've put her back in intensive care. I'll have to go and see what's going on.'

'I'll come with you,' Cass said quickly. 'I need some fresh air.'

Noel looked as if he was going to argue for a moment, but then he nodded. 'Get your coat; it's still freezing out there.'

Ignoring the irritated look on Hector's face, she grabbed her coat and slipped her feet into the fur-lined boots she had left by the back door. She looked at her mother, and Dora nodded. 'Take care, Cassie,' she said.

Hector realised he was outnumbered, and sighed. 'Don't either of you do any experimenting on your own. It could be dangerous.'

Cass saw Noel give Hector a look she couldn't quite interpret. 'I won't let her come to any harm, sir,' Noel said. The added 'sir' was almost insolent, but not quite, and Hector let it ride. Cass picked up her gloves and opened the door, letting in a blast of cold air. She was glad to see it had stopped snowing, but the layer left on the ground was solid ice and she had trouble keeping her feet.

'Thank you,' she said to Noel as she climbed into the car. 'I think that call might have saved us both from a fate worse than death.' She fastened her seatbelt as he reversed down the driveway. 'I thought they were about to let Mary go home. What happened?'

He swung onto the main road and headed in the direction of the hospital. 'I have no idea. It could just be a relapse of some sort. That can happen.'

'But you don't think so?'

'Like I said before, I don't believe in coincidences. She was doing fine until Constantine realised she might be able to help him find the ring. If I'd known that was what he was after, I'd have told him I had it. I didn't mean to put Mrs Shelton in danger. She's been through enough.'

'You can't tell him you have the ring. He'll come after you, and you can't give it to him, however much you want to, because it's stuck on your finger. So what's the point?'

'Because then he'll be hunting *me*, instead of anyone else.'

'If he talks to Mary, she'll tell him she gave the ring to my mother. Then she'll be the one in danger.'

'Exactly. That's why I have to let Constantine know I have it.' He reached across to put a comforting hand on Cass's knee. 'Hector will look after your mother. Together, they make a good team.' He swung into the hospital car park and slapped a police sticker on the windscreen. 'Parking here costs a fortune.'

Cass pulled her coat more tightly around herself as she stepped from the car. A thin, bitter wind was blowing around the hospital building, stirring up little dust devils of powdery snow. Once they were inside she stamped her feet to shake the ice off her boots, then followed Noel across to the reception desk. A woman with bright red lipstick was tapping a computer keyboard.

Noel flashed his badge. 'Mrs Shelton, Mrs Mary Shelton. I believe there's a problem of some sort.' The woman gave Cass the once-over and then looked at Noel enquiringly. 'She's with me,' he said.

The woman tapped her keyboard again. 'Mrs Shelton has been taken to intensive care. They don't allow anyone in there.'

'I understand that,' Noel said patiently. 'But I need to speak to the doctor in charge, or someone else in authority. I was called here by a member the hospital staff, so perhaps you could find that person for me.'

At that moment a rather harassed-looking man appeared round a corner. 'Detective Inspector? Thank you for coming.'

'What happened, Doctor? I saw Mrs Shelton yesterday and she was doing well.'

'Yes, she was. She had been moved to a side room with half-hourly checks.' He looked at the receptionist, who was listening to the conversation with obvious interest. 'I'll take you somewhere we can talk in private.' He led the way to a small room with a few chairs and an examination table, then waved his hand at the chairs and they all sat down. 'My name is Peterson. I'm the registrar in charge of Mrs Shelton's case. She was doing so well that I agreed she could have visitors. She was hoping her son would come to see her. As it was, the only person who came to see her was a man who said he was her brother.'

'Tall and thin, with very pale skin?' Noel asked.

'Yes, that's him. And very strange eyes. Do you know him?'

Noel ignored the question. 'What happened?'

'I have no idea. There was a nursing station right outside the room. The brother came out and told the nurse he was leaving. A few seconds later the alarm went off and it was discovered that Mrs Shelton had stopped breathing. We resuscitated her and I sent her back to intensive care.'

'How is she now?'

'She's been put in a side room and seems back to normal, except for the fact that she can't remember anyone coming to see her, and she tells me she doesn't have a brother.'

'No, she hasn't got a brother,' Noel told the doctor. 'The only family the poor woman has is her son, and he's missing at the moment.' He beamed at Cassandra. 'But Miss Moon is very fond of Mrs Shelton. That's why I brought her with me today. She was devastated by the news that her friend is back in intensive care.'

Cass looked at Noel in surprise, doing her best to look devastated. She was even more surprised when he reached across and took her hand.

I'm going to try to get you in to see her.

It was only because she was looking straight at him that she could see his lips hadn't moved. She clutched his hand more tightly, but he shook his head slightly, and she guessed he hadn't picked up the thought she had tried to send him. If this was only one way, it made things more complicated. She dropped her head, hoping the doctor would think she was crying.

'Miss Moon has been to see Mrs Shelton before,' Noel said to the doctor, 'and I believe the visit benefited Mrs Shelton and helped her progress. The poor woman must be feeling very confused at the moment. A friendly face might restore her memory.'

'I can't see any problem with one visitor; but only one I'm afraid, detective. You'll have to wait here.' He looked at Cassandra. 'A nurse will be present in the room with you, and you'll only be allowed a few minutes.'

Cass nodded and tried to get to her feet, but Noel was still clutching her hand.

See if you can jog her memory.

She pulled her hand away. She wasn't stupid; she would find out everything she could in the time she had. But if Mary couldn't remember Constantine visiting her, there wasn't much she could do.

A nurse was already in the room and she greeted Cass with a smile. 'I'm glad Doctor Peterson let you come up and see Mary. She's getting fed up with being moved around all the time.'

Mary was sitting up in bed, a pink shawl round her shoulders and a welcoming smile on her face. She looked just fine, Cass thought as she sat gingerly on a flimsy plastic chair by the bed. 'What happened to you? I thought you'd be home by now.'

'So did I,' Mary replied. 'They told me I was going home and then I finished up back in that awful place with all the machines. I have no idea what happened. I can't remember a thing.'

'A man came to see you. Do you remember him? He was tall and thin with dark hair and very white skin. Dark eyes, too.'

She shook her head, and then reached for Cass's hand. 'Where's Bradley, Cassandra? Do you know where he is? He'd come to see me if he could. Something bad must have happened to him.'

'That man who came to see you — I think he might know where Bradley is.' Cass was taking a gamble, but she didn't have much time. 'His name is Lucien Constantine. Did Bradley ever mention that name to you?'

Mary pulled herself up in the bed, her eyes suddenly brighter. 'He owns that gambling club, doesn't he? The one Bradley goes to.' When Cass nodded, she sank back down on the bed. 'Bradley was the only one who knew his grandma had that ring. He said she told him he could have it when she died. He asked me to give it to him, but I told him I couldn't find it.' She gave a little sigh, as if her thoughts were painful. 'He didn't have anything to do with my fall, or your mother being taken.'

'Dora's home, fit and well,' Cass said. 'So you don't have to worry about her.' The nurse indicated Cass's time was up, but as she stood up to leave she patted Mary's hand. 'We'll find Bradley for you, Mary, I promise.'

She joined Noel in the waiting area, hoping she could keep her promise.

'Anything?' he asked.

'No, she doesn't remember anyone coming to see her. But she knows Constantine runs a gambling club. She said Bradley had already asked her to let him have the ring, but I think she thought he'd sell it and gamble the money away. She's really worried about him, Noel. I told her we'd get Bradley back for her.'

'I think Constantine told Bradley to ask his mother for the ring, but when he didn't manage to get it Constantine sent in one of his heavies. Mary still wouldn't hand it over, so he pushed her down the stairs and thought he'd killed her. He must have panicked and taken Dora with him because he knew she could identify him.'

Noel waited until Cass was in the car and then started the engine. 'I think you were right. We need to get Bradley out of the club before we do anything else. We can't go in with all guns blazing, not with Bradley still there. He might get caught up in the crossfire.'

Cass looked at him in alarm. 'What crossfire?'

'I was talking figuratively. We should have enough weaponry between us without resorting to guns. I'm sure Hector has a few spells up his sleeve. Your mother can rustle up a jug of poison if we need it, and you can cause an electric storm with your ring.'

'And I can read your thoughts.'

'Yeah,' he said slowly. 'I've had a few ideas about that. We can talk it out when we get back to the house.'

She smiled to herself. They had proved the rings only worked one way, and in a way that was definitely to her advantage. She could read his thoughts, but he couldn't read hers. That suited her just fine.

Noel had work to do, so he dropped her off at the house and disappeared into the evening twilight. Cass couldn't believe how quickly the day had gone. *Time passes quickly when you're having fun*, she thought as she let herself into the warmth of the kitchen. Sometimes she wondered why they had any other rooms in the house, because the kitchen seemed to be the only one they used.

Hector was sitting at the table working on his laptop, while Dora stirred something in a pot on the stove. Cass was never sure if her mother was cooking up a remedy for some strange ailment or preparing the evening meal. She spotted a rabbit skin lying on the worktop and decided the pot probably contained rabbit stew. Hopefully there would also be some of her mother's special herby dumplings simmering in the thick gravy.

Cass pulled off her outer garments and sank onto the sofa. Before she was even settled, Hector handed her a mug of hot tea. 'How is Mary?' he asked.

'Someone visited her in hospital, and just after he left she stopped breathing. She's OK now, but Noel thinks it was Constantine. The problem is, Mary can't remember anything. She can't remember him, or what he said to her, or what she said to him. If he's after the ring . . . ' She hesitated and her mother turned round to look at her.

'Stop worrying about me, Cassie. Mary may have told him she gave the ring to me, but she may also have told him she wanted you to look at it. Constantine knows Hector is back in town, and Noel has visited him in his bat cave.' She smiled. 'So you can be sure he isn't just after me.'

Hector got up and fetched some mats to put on the table. 'Constantine has little power of his own; he relies on his charms and artefacts. There are four of us.' He looked down as the cat nudged his leg. 'And Tobias, of course. I think we'll be more than a match for him.'

'If you're relying on the rings, we may have a problem.' Cass said. 'The power in them only seems to work in one direction. The emerald sends out signals and the sapphire picks them up. A bit like the old crystal radio sets.'

'So nothing magical about it, then?' Hector said with a smile.

Cass frowned at him. 'There is such a thing as science, Father. I don't know whether you've heard about it, but they teach it in schools up and down the country.'

Dora carried her pot of rabbit stew over to the table. 'Well, all the arguments will have to wait until tomorrow. Noel isn't here, so we can't do any experimenting with the rings tonight, and my stew is ready.'

11

Cass looked out of her bedroom window at the garden below. The sun was shining and the snow was melting fast. The privet hedge was sending up wisps of steam in the unexpected warmth, and the few remaining icicles had shrunk to dripping shards. Her bedroom was chilly, but not uncomfortably so, and a quick run to the bathroom meant she was soon under a hot shower. It was a new day, and the world wasn't quite as scary as it had looked last night.

By the time she got downstairs, Hector was scrambling eggs and the kitchen smelt of freshly made coffee. She took bread out of the bin and sliced it for the toaster. The three of them worked silently, like a well-rehearsed team, and she found she quite liked the quiet domesticity. Once the hot toast was buttered, the eggs were placed in a fluffy mound on a heated dish, and she had coffee in front of her, she felt ready to face pretty well anything.

Then Noel breezed in through the outside door and her sense of wellbeing vanished. She scowled at him. 'Don't you have work to do? Solving crimes and things?'

He just grinned at her. 'I love you too.' He filled the plate Dora handed to him with toast and eggs and sat down beside Cass. 'I can't stay long because I really do have work to do, but I agree with you, Hector. We have to test these rings thoroughly and find out exactly what they can do, both together and apart. And then you and Dora need to tell me what powers you both have. We can't take on someone like Constantine unless we know one another's strengths and weaknesses. An emergency number for our mobile phones would be a good idea, too. Some way of contacting one another if we get into difficulties on our own.'

'Eat your breakfast, Noel,' Dora said mildly. 'An army can't fight on an empty stomach.'

'I have to get some work done as well,' Cass said. 'I'm attending a jewellery fair next week, and I have to make some new pieces to take with me. I can't afford to waste any more time.'

Hector handed Noel a mug of fresh coffee. 'This is not a waste of time, and it has to be dealt with, Cassandra. Constantine was just a nuisance, but now he's threatening my family and making it personal.'

Dora looked at him across the table. 'You can't let it become personal, Hector. Your emotions will cloud your judgment.'

'Nothing ever clouds my judgment, Pandora. And, if I remember rightly, you accused me once of not having any emotions.'

'That won't be a problem, then,' she said calmly, as she started to collect the plates. 'Cassie, I think your ring will do anything you want it to, but you have to believe in it.'

Cass closed her eyes. That might be a little too much to ask — too big a step for her to take. It was like asking someone to believe water isn't really wet and fire doesn't burn.

Noel came and stood beside her. 'It's hard for me too. I'm still trying to get used to the idea that you can see inside my head.'

She smiled up at him. 'Only what you want me to see. I'd hate to have to sort through all the other rubbish that must be in there.'

He looked at her thoughtfully for a moment and then bent down so he could whisper in her ear. 'Somewhere in amongst all that rubbish is at least one erotic thought about you, so be very careful where you look.'

She felt her skin heat, absurdly relieved he couldn't read her thoughts. She felt the familiar lightness in her head and mentally cursed him. He knew exactly what he was doing — just waiting for her to literally fall at his feet. Anger pushed the faintness away and she stood up, glaring at him. Why did he do it? Whenever she was feeling really mellow towards the man, thinking she might actually like him, he did something to annoy her.

Hector walked over to join them. 'You were talking about a crystal radio set, Cassandra, and I wondered how far we can take that analogy. Is it possible the emerald might act as a conduit?'

Cass frowned. 'I don't know what you mean.'

'Put your hand on my shoulder,' Hector said to Noel. 'The hand with the ring on it. Then hold Cassandra's hand, again the one with the ring on it.'

'But they aren't touching . . . ' she started to say. Then her eyes opened wide. 'A blue horse?'

Hector smiled at them with satisfaction. 'Exactly as I thought. A conduit. Mind you, I was projecting that thought really strongly. Let's try it with Dora.'

Noel removed his hand from Hector's shoulder and held it out to Dora. She gave her husband a small smile as she took Noel's hand. 'This is all very cosy, Hector.'

Cass shook her head. 'It's like white noise, only it's not a noise. It's a bit like the stuff you get on the screen when the telly's about to pack up.'

Hector frowned at his wife. 'Are you deliberately blocking, Pandora?'

'Of course I am. And Constantine will do the same. You'll only get one chance, and then he'll block you out.'

'Then we'll have to make the most of that one chance.'

Cass pleaded a headache and the need to work. Dora gave her a pill to ward off the headache and she headed to her studio.

The garage conversion was her retreat; somewhere to go when things got too much for her. She picked up a piece of jade and held it in her hand. She had shaped and polished the pale green stone into a perfect teardrop, ready to be hung from a gold chain and sold at the fair next weekend; but for the moment she closed her eyes and absorbed the feeling of calm emanating from the stone. It felt like a cool oasis in the midst of chaos.

* * *

Once Cass had left for her studio, Noel headed back to his office at Norton Police Station. The first thing he'd done when he got out of bed that morning was have another go at removing the ring. It didn't need to anchor itself to his finger like a bright green limpet, he thought irritably. Then he sighed. Yes, it did. If he ever managed to take it off, he might never put it back on again. The idea of magic — the thought that witches and wizards might exist in the normal world — fascinated him. But he was a police detective. His job was to solve crimes here in Norton, not go around reading people's thoughts.

He looked down at his hand,

wondering what other powers the ring possessed. Not that he wanted to try any experiments, but for some reason the green stone had chosen his finger to settle on, and he was still wondering why. He believed he had a much more open mind than Cass, but he still couldn't get his head around the idea of Destiny with a capital 'D'. He had to believe he was master of his own fate. If he had no control over his own life, then he might as well sit down and just let things happen.

Brenda greeted him with yet another cup of coffee, but he took it gratefully. He needed several shots of caffeine to keep him grounded in reality. She had only just left his office when Kevin stuck his head in the door. 'You know that club boss you asked me to check on?'

'Constantine.'

'Yes. He's quite an evasive character, but there's a definite link to a large drug cartel called Manix. The drug boss is Columbian, a guy named Gomez. I found out by chance because I couldn't work out where Constantine got all his money, and I remembered you mentioning drugs. I don't know what Constantine actually does — the club he owns here in Norton runs at a loss — but whatever it is, it's likely funded by this Gomez.'

'Constantine deals in valuable artefacts, which is OK, but the things Constantine goes after are the ones the owners don't want to sell,' Noel explained. 'He encourages his club members to get into debt and then offers to bail them out if they do something for him. Like pushing an elderly lady down the stairs because she wouldn't hand over her husband's emerald ring.'

'The one you're now wearing,' Brenda said as she came back into the room. 'Can I ask why you're wearing it, considering it belongs to Mary Sheldon and should be in the office safe?'

He thought about lying, but what was the point? 'I can't get it off.'

'Can I ask why you . . . ' Brenda began.

'Don't go there,' Noel said warningly. 'This ring is nothing but trouble, and I'd love to get it off, but I can't, so here it will have to stay.'

'Have you tried . . . ' she began again, but the look he gave her had her backing out the door.

Kevin grinned at him. 'D'you want me to have a go?'

'At annoying me, or getting the ring off my finger? I wouldn't suggest either any time soon. Not if you want to keep your job.' Noel walked to his case board, which was now scattered with notes and pictures. 'Do you have any more on our major suspect?'

'Bradley Shelton?' Kevin asked.

'No. I've moved him down the list. I was talking about the man Cassandra Moon saw in the café. Mrs Shelton confirms it was a big man with a bat tattoo who pushed her down the stairs. She got put back in ICU, by the way. It seems someone paid her a visit and she stopped breathing. She's all right now, but she can't remember a thing about her attack or her attacker.'

'So she can't identify anyone?'

Noel shook his head. He wondered how much more he should say. It was difficult to be completely honest with his two detectives without mentioning magic, and he didn't particularly want to lose his job because of suspected mental health problems.

Brenda picked up his mug and headed for the door. 'Want a refill?'

'No thanks, Brenda.'

She pushed open the door with her shoulder. 'I phoned that Constantine person and tried to get a list of club members, but he said he'd already told you the members' names were confidential. Do they have celebrities gambling there, or what?'

Noel laughed. 'I very much doubt a real celebrity would be seen dead in that place. The only reason Constantine won't let me have a list of names is because I asked him for one. I went to see him, thinking the personal touch might work, but he wasn't impressed.'

'Were you wearing that gaudy ring at the time? If so, I'm not surprised. It looks like something out of a Christmas cracker.' Noel thought the ring was rather nice, but he wasn't going to tell Brenda that.

Once they had both left his office, Noel shut the door and turned on his computer. He still had that niggling little thought every time he looked at the ring on his finger. Why him in particular? What was there about him that made him a suitable subject for the ring? There was only one person who might know the answer to that question, and that person was his grandmother.

He picked up the phone and was pleased when she answered almost immediately. He always worried about her when he hadn't spoken to her for some time. His parents had died in a car accident when he was ten years old and his grandmother had brought him up. She only lived an hour away by car, but work prevented him from visiting as often as he wished.

'Noel, how nice to hear from you.'

He loved the warmth in her voice. She always made him feel he was the only person in the world she cared about, and he was sure that was only partly true. His grandmother had time for everyone who crossed her path, particularly any lame duck that might waddle by.

'I was thinking about coming to see you. I can take some time off tomorrow, if that's OK.'

'Of course, dear. Can you come for lunch? I need an excuse to use those apples I picked in the autumn. How does apple pie with cream sound?'

'Would it be all right if I brought a friend with me?'

A picture of Cassandra Moon had suddenly flashed into his mind. He wanted his grandma to meet her. Actually, he thought, he wanted her opinion of the girl he had once almost asked to be his wife.

'Male or female?'

He laughed. 'Female. I'm not gay, Grandma.'

'I was beginning to wonder. A good-looking young man like you and no regular girlfriend. Not that it would make any difference to me. I'm sure gay men like apple pie.'

'I'm sure they do, but I shall be bringing a female friend with me. See you tomorrow.' He hung up before she could ask any more questions. He still had to talk Cassandra into coming with him, but he thought he might put that off for a while.

He was still smarting from his meeting with Constantine. He should have found out more while he was at the club; insisted on seeing Bradley Shelton. It would be a lot more difficult gaining access to the club a second time, he felt sure. Hector seemed to think they could do it, but Noel didn't have Hector's confidence. Perhaps it was because he wasn't a warlock and didn't have Hector's powers.

There were probably things he could do with the ring he hadn't even thought about, but he knew the danger of meddling with things he didn't understand. Was a gemstone that could pick up thoughts any more amazing than a mobile phone? Probably not. As far as he knew, the emerald wasn't much good at sending email or streaming the latest movie. Once you put things in perspective, magic was a bit mundane in the modern world. The paranormal had been forced to take second place to modern technology.

So why, he wondered, was everyone so scared of it?

⋆ ⋆ ⋆

Cass put down the phone down and hurried through the house to the kitchen. 'Noel wants me to go with him to visit his grandmother. He wouldn't take no for an answer. He's coming here tomorrow morning to pick me up.'

She took a breath. 'I shan't go, of course.'

Dora barely looked up from her laptop. 'Whyever not?'

'Because I don't understand why he wants me to go with him. She's *his* grandmother.'

'His parents are both dead, Cassie. His grandmother is all the family he has left.'

'So?' She frowned. 'What's that got to do with me?'

This time Dora did look up, a smile on her face. 'You saw the movie *Meet the Parents*, didn't you?'

'No, no, no!' Cass shook her head violently, her copper hair flying back and forth like a horse's mane. 'If that's what it is, I won't go.'

'Oh, for goodness sake, Cassie, stop behaving like a child. Noel wants you to meet his grandmother. Why is that such a bad thing? Perhaps he just wants some company. Perhaps she's a tyrant and he doesn't want to go on his own.'

'The way he talks about her, she's the most wonderful woman in the world.'

'Well then,' Dora said cheerfully, 'go along and enjoy the ride. I'm beginning to wonder if Noel Raven will ever be able to do anything to please you. Whatever the poor man does, you read some ulterior motive into it.'

'That's right,' Cass said crossly. 'Take his side.'

'Go back and finish your jewellery, Cassie. Your father will be home soon.'

Cass didn't quite storm back to her studio, but almost. She had been having a nice, relaxing afternoon, most of her worries forgotten; but now they had all come rushing back with a vengeance, and all because of Noel Raven. Was she really the bad-tempered bitch her mother had just painted her as? Did she always expect the worst from Noel? Was she scared of visiting his grandmother? Yes to all three, but she didn't quite know what to do about it.

She locked her best stones in the safe and went back to her bedroom. If there wasn't anything better to do, she supposed she could always sort out what she was going to wear to meet Noel's grandmother.

12

'What made you decide to come?' Noel asked. 'I thought you might say no.'

'I nearly did,' Cass replied, 'but my mother told me I was being petty and inconsiderate and my father told me not to be such a baby.'

'So they bullied you into coming?'

'Sort of.' She looked out of the window, interested in a pair of pheasants walking slowly across a field. They obviously knew the open season had ended. 'But I *was* being petty and inconsiderate. It was nice of you to ask me.' A glimpse of the dimple beside his mouth told her he was smiling. 'Why did you ask me to come with you?'

'To stop you being petty and inconsiderate. Oh, and to stop you behaving like a baby. My grandmother is the least scary person you could wish to meet, and her apple pie is to die for.'

He turned his head briefly to look at her. 'I want to ask her some questions about my mother and father, and I need some moral support. Besides that, I don't want to upset her, and you're a good judge of people's moods. If you think she's getting upset, kick me.'

'With pleasure,' she said.

The drive didn't take long, and she was sorry when it ended, but she hadn't expected Noel to drive through double gates into a moss-covered courtyard. An elderly bungalow took up most of the space; an L-shaped ramble of red brick and natural woodwork. The front door was bright cornflower blue, a splash of colour in a bleak, snow-speckled land-scape. Chickens scuttled out of the way as Noel parked the car, and Cass could see a horse poking its head over a stable door.

Noel's grandmother opened her pretty front door before they reached it. She was a tall woman in jeans and a red sweater, her slate-grey hair pulled back in a clip. Cass realised she had heard the words 'grandmother' and 'apple pie' and expected a plump, rosy-cheeked, grandmotherly figure in a flowery apron. This woman looked a lot younger than her 75 years, and there was no sign of the apron.

'I'm Margaret, and I'm really pleased Noel decided to bring a friend,' she greeted Cass. 'I don't usually get to meet his friends.' She stood to one side so they could move into the spacious hallway and hang up their coats. In spite of Margaret's protest, Cass slipped off her boots. The floor looked like polished oak, and if it hadn't been for a circular rug in the middle Cass would have had trouble keeping her feet.

Noel led the way into a large modern kitchen, and Margaret laughed. 'As you can see, Noel always heads for the kitchen. He can smell my apple pie a mile off.' She pulled out chairs for them both at the kitchen table. 'I decided lemonade was too cold, so I spiced a bottle of red wine and heated it up. You must come again in the summer, Cassandra. I have a lovely garden out back and I eat out there whenever the weather is warm enough.'

'Is this a working farm?' Cass asked with interest. She loved the mix of old and new; the bundles of herbs hanging from the ceiling and copper pots on a shelf over the modern range.

'Not really, not anymore. When my husband was alive we ran it as a smallholding, but it was too much for me to manage on my own. Now I grow my own vegetables and keep chickens for their eggs. It's enough to keep me busy. Noel used to love feeding the chickens, and we had several horses then. Now I only have the one I ride myself.' She filled pottery mugs with hot mulled wine and put the steaming jug on the table. 'I made plenty, and diluted it down so it won't make us too tipsy. I know Noel has to drive home later on.' She rested her elbows on the table and looked searchingly at her grandson. 'So what's the purpose of this visit, young man?'

Cass watched Noel fidget in his chair. For a moment he looked like a child about to get a telling-off. 'I told you I missed your apple pie, Grandma. I don't need any more of a purpose than that.'

'But you have one, don't you? Something you want to tell me, perhaps.' She smiled at him slyly. 'I've got a really nice hat.'

Noel looked so bewildered it made Cass laugh. 'We're not getting married,' she said, 'and before you ask, I'm not pregnant either.'

'I'm being incredibly nosy, aren't I?' Margaret said. 'But it's an old woman's prerogative.' She turned her attention back to Noel. 'So why did you come to see me?'

He looked at Cass, but she wasn't sure what he wanted her to say. Margaret was his grandmother and he'd lived with her a long time, so he should know her better than anyone.

'Some things have happened,' he

said. 'Things I need to ask you about. But I don't want to upset you.'

He looked at Cass again, and this time she decided to help him out, even if he didn't like the way she went about it. If she left it up to him, they would be here until midnight. 'Noel wondered if there was anything unusual about his parents,' she said. 'He seems to know very little about them, but he's always been afraid to ask questions in case it upsets you. Recently, some strange things have been happening — to me as well as Noel — and we wondered if these odd occurrences might have anything to do with them.'

Margaret looked at Cass thoughtfully, as if she was weighing her words before she spoke. Eventually she said, 'First of all, it takes a lot to upset me. And why would you think anything that has happened might have something to do with Noel's parents? They've both been dead a very long time.'

'Children inherit certain things from their parents, things that are passed on genetically.' Cass took a deep breath. 'My mother is a witch and my father is a warlock, so I'm used to strange things happening around me. Noel wants to know if he's inherited anything from his parents that might explain a few strange things happening to him.'

Margaret smiled. 'You're Pandora Moon's daughter. I should have realised. I've bought your mother's remedies online for some years.' She looked at her grandson reproachfully. 'You didn't tell me the friend you were bringing to see me was Cassandra Moon.'

'I didn't know it was important,' he said. 'Was my mother a witch, Grandma?'

'No, your mother wasn't a witch. Neither am I. You inherited your abilities from your father. He was a male witch. A wizard, I suppose.'

Noel shot Cass a puzzled look. 'Is that the same as a warlock?'

Cass shrugged. 'Don't ask me. I came into this late as well, remember. I still find it hard to say words like 'witch' and 'wizard', and I'm still not sure I believe any of it.'

'So there's only magic on one side of my family.' He looked at Cass. 'Does that make me a Muggle?'

Cass gave him a withering look. 'It would make you a half-blood, not a Muggle. But you're not Harry Potter, Noel, whatever you might think. You have to take it seriously.'

'I'm trying to. Really, I am trying.'

Margaret emptied the remains of the jug into their glasses. 'I thought you'd start asking questions at some point. I thought it would be sooner than this, to be honest; but you seemed quite normal as a child, and then you joined the police force and did really well, so I put the whole thing out of my mind. Your father was an amazing man, Noel. He had a special gift with animals. A way of communicating with them.'

'Like you do with birds,' Cass told him. 'Now you have the ring, you might find you can really connect with them.'

'I don't particularly want to carry on a conversation with a pigeon.'

'What ring?' Margaret asked.

Noel held out his hand. 'It's not mine. I tried it on and now it won't come off.'

'Have you tried . . . ' Margaret began, but Noel cut her off before she could go any further.

'We've tried everything, Grandma. There's only one thing we haven't tried, and I'm putting that off till the last minute.'

'Your mother hoped your father wouldn't pass on any of his abilities. She wanted you to be a normal little boy without the worry of being different. There can be a dark side to magic, and she wanted to keep you safe and away from all that. When I took over her job of bringing you up, and you didn't show any signs of anything unusual, I thought your mother had achieved her wish.'

'Until now, when you discover I've

been abnormal all along. Sorry, Grandma.'

'I think the word is *paranormal*, not *abnormal*,' she said with a smile. 'But in a way I'm glad you inherited something wonderful from your father. It's a gift, Noel, not a curse, and you must always remember that.'

Cass reached across the table and covered Margaret's hand with her own. 'He isn't alone in this. He has my father and mother to help him — and me.' The phrase came into her mind again: *Together we are invincible*. She squeezed Margaret's hand. 'We make a good team.'

Lunch consisted of a frittata made with fresh farm eggs and served with salad, and they both ate too much of Margaret's apple pie. Cass felt completely relaxed for the first time in weeks. 'Are you sure you're not a witch?' she asked Margaret. 'There is definitely a touch of magic in your cooking.'

'That's my only talent, I'm afraid. I

envy you, Cassandra. I envy all of you. There's so much good you can do with your gifts; I hope you learn to use them well.'

Not for the first time, Cass wondered what it would be like to be normal. Normality had always been her dream, but Margaret had made her realise that without the connection she had with her stones, her life would be very different. It would take her a while to fully accept the gift her parents had given her, but she was beginning to realise how dull things would be without it.

Margaret showed them round the rest of the house, all of it a charming mix of ancient and modern. Before they left she gave them a dozen eggs and a bag of apples to take back to Dora. The light was beginning to fade a little by the time they started for home, but the snow had all gone from the fields, and once they left the country lanes the roads were no problem. Cass settled back in her seat, prepared to enjoy the ride.

The journey home took under an hour, and there was still some light in the sky as they drove through Norton. Noel was about to turn into the drive leading up to the house when a bird landed on the front of the car.

Cass gave a little squeak of fright and Noel almost drove off the road. He had already slowed for the turn and easily brought the car under control, but he looked a little shaken. 'What the . . . ?'

'It was a bird.'

'I know it was a bird. Where did it go? Did I kill it?'

'I don't think so.' Cass undid her seatbelt and slowly got out of the car. 'It's not dead,' she said when she saw the bird sitting on the footpath beside the road. 'Just a little dazed, I think.'

Noel joined her and they both looked down at the bird. 'That wasn't an accident,' he said.

'I know.' Cass bent down and gently lifted the bird. She held it out to Noel. 'Do you think my mother sent it?' The bird wasn't trying to get away. When Noel took it from her it just sat quietly in his cupped hands. *A blackbird*, she thought, looking at its black feathers and bright yellow beak. 'Is my mother in trouble again?'

'I don't know.' He stroked the bird, looking at her helplessly. 'How am I supposed to know what it's trying to tell me?'

She pulled off her glove. 'A conduit, your father said. Hold my hand, Noel.'

He looked at her worriedly. 'Are you sure? Picking up a bird's thoughts could be really weird.'

'We won't know if it will work unless we try, and if my mother is in danger I need to know what's happened.'

Cass didn't know what she was expecting, and for a moment she thought nothing was going to happen — and then her view of the world suddenly changed.

She was in front of Abracadabra, somewhere up fairly high, possibly in a branch of the old oak tree halfway up the drive. A man had just got out of a car parked in the driveway, and was walking towards the house. Her viewpoint changed again and she was moving through the air towards a window. She felt giddy and off balance as the world tilted beneath her, then everything was still again. She saw her mother get up from the kitchen table to answer the door, but there was no sign of her father. She pulled her hand away from Noel's. The flight through the air had been scary and she didn't need to see any more.

'Constantine!' she said. 'He's at the house. My mother is in there alone with Constantine.'

'Where's your father?'

'I don't know, but not in the house.'

Noel put the bird gently on a bank of grass beside the path. 'I'm going to leave the car here where no one can see it and go the rest of the way on foot. Stay here, Cass. I can handle Constantine.'

She gave him a pitying look. 'Stop

trying to be Superman. We work better together. We're a team, remember.' She looked down at her hand where the star in the sapphire pulsed brightly. 'Our charms are gearing up for a fight, and I bet Tobias has his claws out ready for battle.' She was worried about her mother, but apart from that she felt excited. Adrenaline was coursing through her system and all her senses were on high alert. Noel took her hand and the familiar feeling of lightness almost lifted her feet off the ground, but she didn't feel faint this time.

'Are you OK, Cass?'

She smiled at him and pulled her coat more tightly round her body. 'I'm fine.'

'How long has Constantine been in there?' Noel asked as they moved slowly towards the entrance.

Cass hadn't thought of that. There had been no sense of time included with her vision. What she had seen could have happened hours ago, or just a few seconds. 'I don't know for sure, but it felt as if it was happening in real time. We'd better not show ourselves if we can help it. It might be a bit stupid to just march down the drive towards the house. How about we go in the back? If we cut through the trees we can keep out of sight.'

'The trees are bare. They won't give much cover.'

'If we scoot across the entrance one at a time and keep to the right, we can't be seen by anyone looking out of a window.'

Cass glanced at the house as she ran past the opening. There was no sign of Constantine, but she could see a car parked near the front door. They reached the back entrance in a matter of minutes. Dora never locked the door unless she was leaving the house, so Cass assumed it was still open. She looked at Noel and wished he carried a gun, but at least her mother had forewarned them and they knew what they were up against. She wondered how Constantine had managed to get inside the house. Her mother had a safety spell that stopped most things.

She was wondering what to do next when she saw a movement from the trees. Noel turned at the same time, and they both let out their breath together when Hector beckoned to them. 'Constantine is in there,' he told them quietly.

'Yes, we know,' Noel said. 'Dora tipped us off.'

'She knew he was on his way, so I slipped out the back. Dora can manage him for a while. He's always fancied her, so I don't think he'll hurt her.'

'You can't be sure of that,' Cass said worriedly. 'What do you plan on doing next?'

'I was going to wait out here for a bit until we know what Constantine wants. Dora will let me know if she's in trouble. I suggest you go inside, Cassandra, and give Dora some support. Noel can stay out here with me. Let Constantine think Noel just dropped you off and then went on his way.'

She supposed there was some logic in splitting their forces, and there was no point in provoking Constantine unnecessarily. She waited until the two men had moved out of sight, and then opened the door into the kitchen.

Her mother and the lean and handsome Constantine were sitting at the kitchen table drinking mugs of tea. Cass assumed it was tea, because a teapot covered in a knitted cosy had pride of place between them. The little tableau looked calm and peaceful, but Cass could feel the waves of unrest bouncing around the room. She wasn't sure if they were coming from Constantine or her mother.

'Hello, dear,' Dora said. 'Did you have a nice day?'

Cass hadn't exactly expected to find her mother being held at knifepoint, but she hadn't expected her to be having tea with Constantine either.

'Yes, thank you,' she said politely, slipping off her coat and gloves. She warmed her hands at the stove and then turned to face Constantine. 'I presume you have some business with my mother, Mr Constantine.'

'You presume correctly, Miss Moon, and I am pleased you have arrived home so opportunely.' Cass felt like chucking something pointy at the man. He spoke like someone out of a historical novel.

When she didn't answer, he gave her a humourless smile and continued. 'I am in the process of tracking down a particular piece of jewellery — an emerald ring. It is of no particular value in a monetary sense, but it is something I would very much like to add to my collection of antiquities. Your mother suggested it might have passed through your hands recently.'

Cass glared at her mother, who looked back innocently. *Thanks a bundle, Mother*, she thought crossly as she tried to work out what to say without putting anyone in danger. She had a feeling Constantine would know immediately if she tried to lie.

'It might well have passed through my hands, Mr Constantine,' she said, unconsciously mimicking his style of speech, 'but I'm afraid I no longer have it. It was given to me by Mary Shelton for an initial valuation, but then Mary was attacked in her home and I passed the ring over to the local police. I believe it's now locked in the safe at Norton Police Station. I suggest you speak to the detective inspector in charge of the case. His name is Noel Raven,' she added helpfully.

'I see you are still wearing your star sapphire,' Constantine said pleasantly. 'If at any time you feel able to sell it to me, I can assure you of a good price.'

'Cassie won't sell her ring, Lucien. It was given to her by her father.'

Constantine stood up and actually bowed to them both. Cass thought about dropping him a little curtsy, but she managed to restrain herself.

'I must be going, ladies. Thank you for your hospitality, Pandora. I've missed our little chats. I'm sorry Hector is absent.' He smiled. His eye teeth were a little too long, and Cass thought he looked exactly like her concept of a vampire — but she had a feeling that was exactly how he wanted to appear. 'Hector seems to be very adept in avoiding me.'

'I'm sure it isn't intentional,' Dora said. 'He told me he was looking forward to meeting you. I'm sorry I couldn't help you with your search for the emerald ring. You'll have to take my daughter's advice and visit the police station.'

Like hell he will, Cass thought as she saw him out of the front door. Almost immediately, Noel and Hector let themselves in through the back.

'Was he looking for the ring?' Hector asked. 'I thought that was what he'd come for. That's why we kept well away from the house.'

'The stupid thing was hardly helping,' Noel said. 'It was sitting on my finger lit up like a beacon.'

'This whole business is getting out of

hand.' Hector refilled the kettle and switched it on. 'Mary will be out of hospital any day now, and Constantine will almost certainly go after her again. We also have to get her son out of Constantine's clutches.'

Noel nodded. 'We not only have to get Bradley out of there, but we also have to find evidence of drugs, or something else illegal, so we can close the club for good.'

'He'll open one up somewhere else,' Cass said. 'He'll keep the little extortion game going for as long as he can, getting his club members into serious debt and then offering to bail them out for a little favour. When you think about it, it's pretty damn clever. If they don't get into debt, he can hold them to ransom with an offer of drugs.' She emptied the teapot and rinsed it out with boiling water before dropping in a handful of teabags. 'Sometimes that man scares me enough to make my knees knock, and at other times he just seems a little silly.'

'That's another of his tricks, Cassandra, so don't be fooled,' Hector told her. 'Lucien Constantine is one of the most dangerous men I've ever had the misfortune to meet. It will take all our combined energy to defeat him.'

Cass thought her father was being a little melodramatic. Sitting at a table drinking tea with her pretty mother, she wondered if some of Hector's intense dislike of the man could be caused by jealousy. She poured tea for all of them, wrapping her still-cold hands round her mug. The feeling of elation had gone and she just felt empty. She liked Noel's grandmother — she couldn't remember her own — and it would have been nice to think she was going to see Margaret again; but when she had said there wasn't going to be a wedding, Noel had made no attempt to correct her. She wondered how much longer she could continue holding his hand without him finding out she was in love with him — something she had only admitted to herself in the last few hours.

13

There was no watertight plan for getting Bradley out of Constantine's clutches. Noel wanted to go alone to check the place out and see if there was a way in that didn't involve walking in the front door, but Cass thought Noel should stay well away. If Constantine saw the emerald, Noel would be in real trouble.

'I'll wear gloves until I get inside,' he said. 'It's cold enough so they won't look out of place. I'm the only one of us with a plausible reason to pay Constantine another visit. I'll go fairly late tonight and tell him we have reason to believe drugs are being used on the premises. I don't have to accuse him of anything, just ask politely if I can have a look round while the club is open.'

'And you think he's actually going to

give you a guided tour?' Cass looked at him in disbelief. 'He'll spot your ring and know we're on to him.'

'Noel can keep one hand in his pocket,' Hector suggested. 'I'll stay close by and monitor what's going on inside the club. I have access to normal spying equipment. Noel can wear a mike. I promise you, the new technology is undetectable.'

Cass felt a slightly hysterical giggle bubbling up inside her. She was in the company of a witch, a warlock, and a couple of magical gemstones — and Hector was talking about using a wire. He caught her disbelieving look and smiled at her.

'We don't live in a separate universe, Cassandra. Magic and technology go hand in hand in the modern world.' He paused for a few seconds, and then obviously made up his mind about something. 'However, I think you should be nearby as well. Your ring may be able to connect with the emerald at a distance if the circumstances warrant it.

Magic isn't a predictable science. It has the ability to change, depending on the situation at the time.'

'So in other words, you haven't a clue what will happen?'

This time he smiled with genuine amusement. 'That just about sums it up, Cassandra. Thank you for putting everything in perspective.'

Dora had been stirring something on the stove, but now she turned to look balefully at her husband. 'I won't be left out of this, Hector,' she said firmly. 'I know you like to keep me safe, but you of all people should know my strengths. You may have to hang around outside that club for quite some time, in the dark and with the temperature below freezing. At least I can keep you all warm.'

'I know you can look after yourself, Pandora, but it would be stupid to put all our lives in danger if there's no need.'

'There's always safety in numbers. You know that.'

'Apart from your magical powers, Dora,' Noel said, 'a flask of tea and a picnic basket wouldn't go amiss. I doubt I'll get offered any refreshments.'

'There's no point in getting there too early.' Dora took some risen dough out of the warming drawer and started forming it into balls. 'Hot bread rolls and fresh tomato soup will keep us all going for quite a while, and we've still got plenty of time to eat before we leave.'

Cass was beginning to realise they were all taking this quite seriously, and something was actually going to happen that night. She had been thinking it was just speculation, a make-believe scenario that would never take place.

They were all quite mad, of course. Any minute Hector would suggest they camouflage themselves and paint their faces black, like ninjas going into battle. All quite ridiculous. She glared at her father. 'Are you actually going to let Noel go into that club alone?'

Noel frowned at her. 'Believe it or

not, I have been trained to handle myself in difficult situations, Cass. I shall just look around the club and get an idea of the layout.'

'So it's just a reconnaissance?'

He looked uncomfortable. 'Well, obviously, if I spot drugs being used, or see a way of getting Bradley out . . . '

She could see he was getting angry with her, but she couldn't stop herself. She was sure Noel was going to get hurt, and she couldn't imagine her life without him. Somehow she had to think of a way to keep him close, because that was the only way she could keep him safe. 'I don't think splitting up is a good idea,' she said boldly. 'Why don't we go as two couples having a night out? Constantine won't believe a word of it, of course, but he can hardly refuse to let us in, and at least we'll all be together.'

'He can't watch all of us at once,' Dora agreed. 'We can take it in turns to wander off and poke into all the club's dark corners. For all we know, Bradley may be staying there of his own accord. If so, he shouldn't be hard to find.'

It was Hector's turn to look uneasy. He obviously didn't want to have a fight with his wife in front of them, but it was also obvious he didn't want her anywhere near Constantine. 'I don't think either of you two women . . . ' he began, his voice tapering off when Cass and her mother both turned to face him together.

'Are you suggesting we can't take care of ourselves?' Dora asked fiercely. 'I can do more than make potions and keep myself warm, Hector. I've proved that many times. I think Cassie's idea is excellent. At heart, Lucien is a coward. I don't think he'll be able to cope with all of us together. I think we'll scare him to death just by being there.'

'Don't underestimate him, Pandora.'

'I would never underestimate him, but he has no power of his own, and most of the trinkets he's managed to acquire won't work for him. He has the handle of a staff that belonged to

257

Merlin — something I've always coveted — but all he can do is take it out of his safe and look at it from time to time. He has no idea what to do with it.'

'I thought Merlin was a legend?' Cass said.

Dora laughed. 'In that case, so is Constantine.'

No one mentioned any plans for the evening until dinner was over. Cass had a feeling Hector was avoiding the issue. Perhaps he thought if he kept quiet the two men could slip out unnoticed, but Cass knew her mother was watching them surreptitiously. She helped Dora clear the table and pour the coffee. 'What time should we leave?' she asked. 'We need time to change before we go out. We have to look as if we're intent on having a good time.'

'Constantine won't believe that for a minute.' Hector looked at her over the top of his coffee mug.

'I know he won't believe it.' Cass smiled at her father. 'But the other members of the club won't know we're imposters, will they? He won't have time to warn them because he'll be trying to watch all of us at once, so someone might let slip where Bradley is.'

'We do have a secret weapon,' Noel said. 'If Cass is with me, I just have to ask the right questions to get the right answers.'

Hector sighed. 'It looks as if I'm outvoted on this. I can see the logic of Cassandra's plan, but it'll be distracting if I'm trying to keep you women safe.'

Does it count as abuse if you hit your father? Cass wondered. Because she was getting really close to taking a swipe at Hector. Why did he think he had to keep them safe? He had been missing for nearly thirty years of her life, and it was a bit too late now to make up for lost time. She had learned to look after herself the hard way. His overprotectiveness was either a result of his job, or maybe a guilty conscience. If a person's aim in life was to keep the world safe, they probably would get a bit paranoid about their own family.

Dora's idea of dressing up was to wear a silver caftan decorated with tiny beads that changed colour when she moved. If she was hoping to draw attention to herself, the caftan would certainly do that. Cass thought her mother looked like a tiny, ethereal rainbow, the delicate colours flickering in and out of existence as she walked across the room. Cass had made an effort, but she had approached it with a little more subtlety. She had chosen a pair of black leather jeans bought in a moment of madness, and a clingy cornflower-blue top.

She smiled when Noel let out a soft wolf-whistle. 'You see?' she said. 'You men should be able to go wherever you want at the club. No one will be looking at you.' She was wearing the sapphire earrings her mother had given her for her birthday; her only other jewellery was the star sapphire on her right hand. Her copper hair had been pulled up into a loose chignon and secured with a silver comb. She wasn't used to dressing up, but she felt pretty good about herself. She had opted for low-heeled ankle boots rather than high heels, because she didn't know when she might need to break into a run or leap out of the way of a lightning bolt.

Noel was still wearing his jeans, but now they were teamed with a long-sleeved T-shirt borrowed from Hector. Cass thought her father looked positively formidable in a black jacket and charcoal shirt open at the throat. She caught a glimpse of an amulet on a gold chain, and wondered if it was a charm of some sort. She couldn't imagine him going into a fight empty-handed.

They piled into Hector's big four-by-four rather than take one of the smaller cars. Again, speed and versatility might come in handy at some point. The car was warm in minutes — the result of an efficient heater or a spell from Dora, Cass didn't really care which. She had put all her reservations on hold for the evening. She even gave her sapphire a rub before she clicked on her seatbelt. Every little bit of help would be welcome.

Hector handed out visitors passes. 'Constantine might query them if he's on the door, but I don't think he will be. A doorman's job is beneath him. He'll be working one of the gambling tables, or watching the players from a secret hidey-hole somewhere in the building.'

'So he'll know we've arrived?' Cass asked.

'Of course he'll know, but once we're inside there's nothing he can do about it without making a scene, and he won't want to do that.'

There were a number of cars parked outside the Bat Club, and Cass felt her breath hitch. It was all very well talking about taking on Constantine, but she had met the man and knew the fear he could generate. She was ready to grab Noel's hand if she felt threatened in any way, but she didn't have to worry, as he took her hand in his as soon as they were out of the car.

'It's a good way of hiding the ring,' he said. 'If I say something aloud in my head, you'll know what I'm thinking. I promise I won't think lewd thoughts about you, even though you look amazing.'

She cocked her head to one side. 'All I can hear is white noise.' She smiled at him. 'And now I can see a picture of a raven.'

'I'm getting much better at blocking.' He squeezed her hand. 'All geared up and ready to go, then.'

★　★　★

Noel realised it had been easy to tell Cass he wouldn't think about her, but much harder to put into practice. She looked stunning. The leather jeans accentuated some attractive features he hadn't noticed before, and he had to keep running through a list of birds in his head so she couldn't pick up his real thoughts. For days he had been wondering what it would be like to be married to her, but the time to tell her had never seemed quite right.

Hector handed over their passes and the man guarding the door nodded, waving them through. Hector had managed to add their names to the guest list using his laptop, but the doorman was more interested in giving Cass the once-over than checking his list. Noel managed to resist the temptation to inflict bodily harm. He knew the poor man couldn't help himself.

The club was crowded, but Noel had expected that. It was a Saturday night, and there were a number of women present wearing everything from tattered jeans to dresses that stopped just short of indecency. For the men, jeans appeared mandatory. Hector was the only male Noel could see wearing a suit. Until Lucien Constantine strode into view dressed all in black.

Cass still had her hand tucked in

Noel's. He could feel a small tickle of electricity when the rings touched, and realised in that instant that his emerald could do far more than just read thoughts, particularly when it was linked with Cass's sapphire. *Together we are invincible*. He certainly hoped so.

Constantine was having difficulty hiding his annoyance, but Noel could also see fear in those black eyes. He felt a buzz of power as he held out his right hand to him. 'This is a purely social visit, Mr Constantine. We're having a little celebration, and this seemed the perfect place for an evening out.'

Constantine took his hand and gripped it a little too firmly, putting uncomfortable pressure on his knuckles. Childish, but effective. 'A celebration? How nice. May I ask the nature of this special occasion?'

Noel had to think fast. He had no idea why he had told Constantine they were celebrating something. It had seemed a good reason for them all to be at the club, but now he had to come up with something plausible. He gave Cass's hand a gentle squeeze and jumped in with both feet. 'Earlier this evening I asked Cassandra Moon to marry me, and she said yes. Perhaps you could find us a table, Mr Constantine, and ask someone to bring a couple of bottles of champagne.'

'Of course. You are welcome to as much champagne as you can drink, all on the house. Call it a small engagement gift.' He lifted Cass's free hand. 'No engagement ring yet, Miss Moon?'

Noel winced as she pulled her hand back. 'It was all rather sudden, Mr Constantine, but I'm sure Noel is going to buy me something really beautiful. I have a rather large diamond in mind.'

Touché. Noel wanted to tell her he meant every word of it, and if she wanted a big diamond, he'd get her the biggest he could afford. But Hector had already moved forward and was now nose to nose with Constantine.

'Lucien, good to see you at last. I've

been inordinately busy recently, away most of the time, or I would have called in sooner. I didn't realise you were the new owner of the Bat Club. Doing well, is it?'

'Exceptionally well, thank you.' Constantine smiled at Dora. 'You look particularly beautiful tonight, Pandora. I can't tell you how much I enjoyed our little chat together this afternoon. If you'd told me you were planning on coming here tonight, I could have given you all passes. It would have saved Hector having to forge them.' This time the smile was for Hector. 'If you'd care to come with me, I can offer you a table in a private room.'

Constantine had already turned his back and started across the room, but Hector held up his hand to stop them following. 'Thank you, Lucien, but we'll take that empty table in the corner. Tonight is a celebration and we want to be in the thick of things, not tucked away in a back room.'

Where you can keep an eye on all of

us, Noel thought. Constantine might be clever, but he was human and, as far as Noel knew, limited to human capabilities. No match for the witches and wizards of this world. That was what he hoped, anyway.

Cass stopped him taking her hand as they sat down, but she stayed next to him, her hand in easy reach. He tucked one hand in his pocket to keep the emerald out of sight. 'It feels quite strange being engaged to be married,' she said, 'particularly when I haven't actually had a proposal, but I suppose you had to think up a reason for us all being here together. As reasons go, it was quite a good one, even if you didn't mean a word of it.'

Noel realised they were all looking at him. This wasn't how it was supposed to happen. He had been thinking of a candlelit dinner where she'd know exactly what he was trying to say. Spelling out how he felt about her in a sleazy nightclub in front of her mother and father wasn't an option he would have chosen. He cleared his throat, hoping his voice didn't squeak like it sometimes did if he was nervous. He wanted to hold her hand again, but he could feel sweat lining his palm. He rubbed his hand on his jeans and cleared his throat again.

'I meant every word of it, Cassandra, except for the fact that it all happened in the wrong order. Normally I would have waited until you said yes before I invited you mother and father to our engagement party.' He was glad the lighting was dim enough to hide most of his embarrassment. 'I want to marry you. I fell in love with you the first time I saw you, but to be honest, I was scared. Your family isn't exactly normal, and I thought mine was very ordinary. I didn't think I could ever fit in.' He waited until she turned to look at him and he could see himself reflected in those gorgeous amethyst eyes. 'But now I know I'm the same as the half-blood prince, I feel worthy of you.' He pulled a little box out of the pocket of his jeans and handed it to her. 'I bought this a few days ago, before I found out you wanted a big diamond, so I hope you like it.'

He had taken a gamble, and he sighed with relief when she smiled. There was no ring in the box, just a perfect blood-red ruby cut in the shape of a heart. 'I saw this,' he told her with a smile, 'and thought of you. It was a ruby that brought us together in the first place.'

Cass turned to kiss him lightly on the lips. 'It's quite beautiful, and absolutely perfect. I don't really like diamonds. And because you may still want it official, the answer is yes, I would love to marry you, Noel Raven. I thought you'd never ask.'

Dora was on her feet before Noel had finished speaking. She gave him a hug and kissed his cheek. 'I've always wanted a son.'

Hector patted him on the shoulder. 'I know you'll look after her, Noel. This had to happen. You belong together.'

Someone brought champagne to the table and filled Noel's glass, but all he wanted to do was look at Cass. He had imagined that once she said yes, she would be his, but he knew she would never belong to him. They were destined to become a team, and he could live with that; but all he wanted to do right now was get her somewhere on her own so he could show her exactly how much he loved her.

'I hate to break up the party,' Hector said apologetically, 'but we're here for a reason. We have a job to do. We still have to find Bradley.'

'I've been keeping my eyes open in spite of all the excitement,' Dora said. 'If I walk around pretending I'm looking for the ladies' room, I might be able to sense something. At the moment all I'm picking up is the love and happiness at this table.'

Noel took Cass's hand and pulled her to her feet. 'We'll take a look at the gambling tables and ask a few questions. Someone must know something.'

'And I'll keep an eye on Constantine,' Hector said, 'although actually he's in a better position to watch all of us.' He looked up at the ceiling. 'He's got cameras everywhere.'

Noel didn't care about the cameras. He didn't have to pretend anymore. He put his arm round Cass's slim waist and pulled her against him. Whatever Constantine might throw at them, he had a feeling they were going to come out of it OK.

14

The gaming tables were in a back room. Baccarat and roulette were being played at the two main tables, while card games were in progress in smaller groups at the edge of the room. Cass didn't like gambling, and she suggested to Noel they would be more likely to pick up information at the bar. At least there would be no problem about making bodily contact with the crowd waiting for drinks. Noel was having trouble pushing his way to the front without letting go of her hand.

'Hang on to me, darling,' Noel said, raising his voice slightly. 'It looks like we'll be here a while.'

She caught his thought immediately. 'I haven't seen Bradley Shelton, have you? I thought he was always here on a Saturday night.'

'He might be at one of the tables. We'll get a drink first and then go and look for him.' He rested his hand lightly on the arm of the man in front of him. 'Excuse me, mate. You haven't seen Bradley around, have you? He said to meet him here.'

A quick flash of Bradley with Constantine, then it was gone. Cass thought Constantine looked as if he was having an argument with Bradley, but the picture was gone before she could really latch on to it. The man in front had turned round and Noel had to let go of his arm.

'Sorry,' the man said. 'Sometimes he comes in, sometimes he doesn't. I haven't seen him for a while now, maybe a week. You could ask Ted, he knows Brad better than me.'

The man had pointed to someone at the other end of the bar — a large man, still looking as irritable as he had in the café.

Cass pulled Noel away from the bar. 'That's him,' she whispered. 'The big man from the café with the bat tattoo on his wrist.'

'Most of the people in here will have a tattoo of a bat on them somewhere,' he said.

'No, I recognise him. He's the man who took my mother.'

Noel grinned at her. 'Now we're getting somewhere. Between us we should be able to rattle him. You tell him you recognise him from the café, and then I'll tell him I'm a policeman looking for Bradley. That should do the trick.'

'If you tell him you're a policeman, he'll clam up.'

'His brain will be on fire trying to work out how much we know, so he won't be able to keep his thoughts hidden. I've just got to think of a way to hang on to him while you try to pick up something relevant.'

They were about to make their way to the other end of the bar when Dora appeared beside them. 'There's an annex out the back,' she said. 'A block of motel-type rooms, some with cars parked outside. I couldn't think of a reason to walk across the courtyard and listen at the doors, but if Lucien has Bradley, I'm willing to bet he's in one of those rooms.'

'Don't look now,' Cass said, with a nod towards the end of the bar, 'but is that the man who kidnapped you?'

Dora's eyes opened wide. 'I'm surprised he has the gall to show himself. He must know I'd recognise him if I saw him again.'

'But this is the last place he'd expect to see you, Dora,' Noel said. 'He'd think he was safe in here with all his cronies. Besides, it's your word against his. In court, they'd argue that you can't see more than two inches in front of your face and your memory is going because of your age.'

Cass was still watching the big man. 'What if we all confront him at once? I think he might fall apart. Coming face to face with the woman he left to die in the snow is bound to be a bit stressful, isn't it?'

'Where's Hector?' Noel asked.

Dora looked round the room. 'Goodness knows. He's keeping an eye on Constantine, so he could be anywhere.'

Cass checked the bar to make sure the man was still there. He obviously hadn't seen them or he'd be miles away by now. 'I'll speak to him first, say I recognise him from the coffee shop, and then Noel can step in. We'll keep Dora as our ultimate weapon.'

Dora wiggled with delight, her silver hair floating round her shoulders. 'I like the sound of that. Let me know if you want me to blow him up.'

Cass frowned. She had a feeling her mother was serious. With a last squeeze of Noel's hand, she left them and walked the length of the bar. Someone couldn't resist a low wolf whistle, and the big man stopped talking to his friend and turned to look at her. He looked faintly puzzled, as if he half-remembered seeing her somewhere before.

She carried on going as if she was

going to walk on past, but at the last minute she stopped in front of him. 'I thought I recognised you.' She tried a seductive smile, a novelty for her, but it must have worked because his friend leered at her.

'Don't you recognise me as well?' the friend asked. He was short, with a bald head and sweat patches under his arms. 'I'm sure we've met before. Probably in my dreams.' He laughed at his own joke and then poked his friend in the ribs. 'Well, introduce me.'

Cass forced herself to smile at the sweaty little man. 'I don't think your friend remembers me.' She turned her attention to the big man. 'You were in the coffee shop in town on that awful snowy morning. I remember you because you seemed in a hurry to get away.'

The man looked a little nervous. He clearly didn't want anyone to remember him. But he didn't want to turn down a sure thing, either. 'How could I forget?' he said with a smirk. 'I remember all the beautiful girls.'

'Do you, now,' Noel said, coming up behind them and sliding a possessive arm round her waist. 'So you know my fiancée, do you?'

Noel was as tall as the tattooed man but not as heavily built. He was leaner and fitter, and Cass would definitely put her money on him if it came to a fight.

'We were just talking,' the big man said. 'Your woman, is she?' Sorry, mate, I didn't know.'

Cass really wanted to hit the idiot, but they needed information. 'Actually,' she said, her voice tinged with ice, 'I'm not anyone's woman. This is Noel Raven. He's a police detective.' A double whammy, she thought gleefully when she saw the mixed emotions flitting across the man's face. His friend had backed off, obviously realising that he was outclassed all the way down the line.

The big man, however, wasn't as sensible. 'I'm surprised the boss let you in. He doesn't like the law poking around.'

'Yes, it surprised me as well,' Noel said. 'You wouldn't think he'd want a policeman anywhere near the place, considering the line of work he's in. Gambling and drugs — not a good combination as far as the law is concerned.'

Dora timed her appearance well. She came up behind Cass and tugged at her daughter's arm. 'That's him!' She hissed the words in a loud stage whisper that carried all the way up the bar.

Cass turned round, pretending surprise. 'What are you on about, Mother?'

'The man who kidnapped me. The man who left me in that old house without any heat or food, Cassie. He left me to die!'

Noel took the opportunity to put his hand on the big man's arm. 'The same man who nearly killed Bradley's mother? Are you sure?'

Cass caught the thought in flickering pictures. Bradley in a shouting match with the big man, Constantine coming into the picture to break it up.

'Stupid old woman.' The man shook himself free from Noel's grip. 'She doesn't know what she's talking about.'

'Where's Bradley Shelton?'

Cass shook her head. The man didn't know. He had seen Constantine lead Bradley away, and then she received nothing but mix of disjointed thoughts turning into a flickering snowstorm.

The big man glowered at Noel. 'How would I know? I'm not bloody psychic, am I?'

'I should be very careful what you say,' Noel warned. 'I already have enough to take you in for suspected abduction, and that 'stupid old woman' is my fiancée's mother.'

Cass thought it might spoil things if she laughed, but she could see from her mother's face that Noel should have chosen his words with more care. She looked at the sweating man and decided to try a different tack. 'If you help us find Bradley,' she said kindly, 'it'll prove he's still alive. My boyfriend thinks he was murdered by the same man who took my mother. They both went missing at the same time, you see.'

'Hang on,' the man said, his voice going up a notch. 'I didn't kill no one.'

She wanted to point out that if he 'didn't kill no one', he obviously killed *someone*, but she thought now might not be a good time for a grammar lesson.

'Oh my goodness!' Dora put both hands up to her face. 'Did this man murder Bradley? My best friend's son? Oh, how awful!' She sagged against Noel as if she might fall, and he put an arm round her.

'We have to find somewhere she can sit down,' Noel told the big man. 'But I know who you are and where you live. I shall expect to see you in the police station tomorrow morning. If you don't come in of your own accord, I shall send someone to get you.' He hiked Dora to her feet and half-carried her away from the bar.

'You can walk now, Mother,' Cass said sharply once they were out of earshot of the two men. 'You don't need to overdo it.'

Hector was beside them before they reached their table. 'What happened?' he asked Noel. 'Is Dora hurt?'

'No, I'm fine,' she told him with a smile. 'Just play-acting.'

Hector opened the second bottle of champagne. 'Either drink it, or water the plastic flowers with it. This is supposed to be a celebration.'

'We'll celebrate properly once this is over.' Cass looked at her mother. 'Have you sniffed out any drugs in your travels?'

'I'd only smell a restricted drug it if it was plant-based, like cannabis. I can't help you find pills or hard drugs.'

'We need a warrant to search the place,' said Noel, 'but if Constantine is holding Bradley against his will, that should be enough.' He looked at the door leading to the gaming room. 'If there was a commotion at one of the tables, Constantine would have to go and sort it out. That might give us enough time to check out the annex at the back.'

'I'll do it.' Dora held up her purse. 'I've got enough money to buy some chips, and I've already got a reputation as a silly old woman. They'll welcome me to one of the card tables.'

Noel gave her a worried look. 'Are you sure you want to do this, Dora? It could get nasty.'

'Then I'll call for help. Hector will know if I need him.'

Hector nodded. 'You two can have a look at the cabins while I keep an eye on Pandora. Don't do anything, mind. This is just a reconnaissance. Report back here to me as soon as you can.'

Without another word, Dora left them and made her way past the roulette wheel to one of the smaller card tables. Someone immediately offered her a seat, and Cass smiled to herself. If the people seated round the table thought Pandora Moon was just a silly woman, they were in for a nasty shock. Cass let Noel top up her glass, even though she had no intention of drinking any more champagne, and then they waited in expectant silence.

The volume of sound began to rise after about five minutes. Several voices were raised in anger, and Cass got to her feet and casually wandered over to look into the room. Dora was calmly scooping gaming chips into her capacious handbag while two of the men shouted at her. She caught sight of her daughter and winked.

'Time to move,' Cass told Noel. She didn't know how long Dora could keep the players occupied, but she suspected they would want to win their money back. 'I think my mother can keep them entertained long enough for us to have a look at the cabins.'

'How does she manage to win?' Noel asked curiously. 'She's not telepathic, is she?'

'She can't read thoughts,' Cass said. 'But she's always been able to pick up people's moods. Very handy in a game of chance. Excitement is very different from a feeling of anxiety, and Dora can spot that difference. A poker face won't work with her.'

Hector moved to another table where he could watch Dora without looking obvious. 'Constantine has just turned up. He may suspect Pandora of causing the commotion, but she'll slip away before he can do anything about it. I'll keep her safe, but I can't watch over you two at the same time. Find out if Bradley is in one of those cabins, but don't do anything to attract attention.'

'My father does have a habit of repeating himself,' Cass muttered.

They split up and went in different directions to confuse the cameras before meeting up in the courtyard. The space in front of the cabins was well-lit, but Noel waved his hand at the overhead light and somehow managed to plunge the whole area into darkness. Cass couldn't see his face, but she thought he was probably as surprised as she was.

Initially all the cabins had looked unoccupied, but now Cass could see a streak of light coming from behind a closed blind. She slipped silently across the open space, with Noel following her. She wished he hadn't turned the light out. If there was something nasty lurking nearby she'd prefer to see it coming, rather than have it jump out of the dark at her. All her senses were on high alert. Adrenalin was pumping through her veins and her heart was bumping against her ribs. She glanced down at her ring, but the blue star wasn't giving her any hint of immediate danger.

Noel put his hand on her shoulder from behind and she almost screamed. She turned round, intending to tell him off for scaring her, but he covered her mouth with his before she could speak. 'I love you, Cassandra Moon,' he said softly a few moments later. 'I wanted to tell you before I lost my chance.' He pulled her even closer, wrapping his arms around her as if he was scared she might slip away. 'I'm going to do my best to keep you safe, but I'd much rather you turned around and went back to the bar. I'm pretty sure you won't do that, so I need a moment alone with you in the dark.'

The moment turned into several minutes before she reluctantly pulled away. She could feel the electricity singing in her veins, but it was a pleasant tingle; something she could easily get used to. 'We can't stay here too long, Noel,' she whispered. 'Someone will notice the light's out and come looking.'

They moved up tight against the cabin wall beside the lighted window, too close now to risk even a whisper without the chance of being heard by someone inside. Cass needed to know if Noel had a plan.

As if he was reading her thoughts, Noel took hold of her hand. *Can you see anything through the cabin window?*

She pressed her face against the

glass, but the gap in the blind was too small. When she shook her head, he bent down and put his ear against the door. After a couple of seconds he stood up and turned to look at her.

There's someone in there. I can hear them moving around.

She couldn't answer him and she had no idea what he wanted her to do next, but there was no point standing in the dark outside the cabin. Without looking at him again, she took a deep breath and knocked on the door. There was the noise of scuffling inside and the sound of people speaking, but she couldn't hear what was being said. Eventually the door opened a crack.

'Yes?' The man was wearing unzipped jeans and an inside-out T-shirt, and he looked annoyed. Cass got a glimpse of a rumpled bed and a bare leg. The leg looked female. Noel stayed out of sight, leaving Cass to do the talking.

'Sorry to disturb you,' she said. 'I'm looking for Bradley Shelton. I thought this was the number he gave me.'

The man's initial annoyance seemed to have gone. He gave her a slow once-over and a rather nauseating leer. 'Brad's a lucky man. Come back if you can't find him.' He glanced over his shoulder. 'I'll have finished with this one by then.'

Cass had an urgent desire to move as far away from the man as she could, but she bravely stood her ground. 'Do you know where Bradley is?'

Cass decided the second leer was worse than the first. 'You don't need him, sweetheart,' the man said, 'I can give you a much better time.'

She felt Noel twitch beside her. 'No thank you,' she said politely, trying to avoid a punch-up. 'Are any more of these cabins occupied, do you know?'

The man shook his head. 'No idea. Look, lady, I only rented this one for an hour, so I might as well make the most of it.' Another look over his shoulder. 'Unless you fancy a threesome. She won't mind.'

Cass thought the woman on the bed had probably gone to sleep, but she was sure Mr Sleazy would soon wake her up.

Almost before the door had shut, Noel had taken Cass's hand and pulled her away. She could sense his mood was more angry than anxious. He was furious with the sleazy man for daring to make a pass at her.

'What are you so stirred up about?' she whispered when they were far enough away from the line of cabins not to be overheard. 'Did you think I was going to say yes to his suggestion?'

'Of course not.'

'In that case, you'll have to trust me to make my own decisions, or we're going to have a problem. I don't want you snorting with anger every time another man looks at me.' She stood still and reached up to cup his face in her hands. 'I love you, Noel. I don't want anyone else, and I'm pretty sure it will always be that way.'

He kissed her lightly. 'Sorry, but I

think you might feel the same if I'd been chatting up that half-naked woman on the bed.'

Half-naked? Cass hadn't noticed the woman was half-naked, but Noel obviously had. 'Shall we check the rest of the cabins?' she asked.

They moved down the row, giving a gentle tap on the door of each one. All the cabins remained dark and silent. Cass held back at the last cabin. Something wasn't right. Her ring tingled on her finger, sending a fizz of electricity up her arm. She took hold of Noel's hand.

Someone in there?

She couldn't answer him without being heard, so she nodded. He moved closer to the door and lowered his head to listen, his ear pressed against the woodwork. He was off balance, and when the door suddenly opened he practically fell inside. Cass wanted to run, but she couldn't leave Noel, and before she could make a decision the light came on.

Constantine seemed to fill the doorway. The light was behind him and his face was in shadow, but she could see the look of glee in those dark, dark eyes, and her blood froze.

15

Without waiting to be asked, Noel walked inside the cabin. Cass followed, even though every nerve in her body was urging her to run.

Go and get help, you idiot.

The words were loud and clear in her head, but her heart wouldn't let her leave.

'So, I have you both together. That will save some time. I should have guessed you'd work as a pair. Was all this about an engagement really true, or just a ploy to get inside my club?'

When neither of them answered, he smiled. 'It really doesn't matter. No amount of love can get you out of this predicament.'

Noel made a lunge for Constantine but he never made contact. Cass watched in dismay as Noel shot backwards and hit the cabin wall. He kept his feet, but he looked stunned.

'Just a small charm I picked up.' Constantine held up a small gold amulet he had been concealing in his hand. 'It's not a weapon exactly, but very good protection, so don't try that again, Detective, unless you want to get hurt. All I want is the ring you are wearing. I spotted it on your finger in the club.' His eyes glistened. 'Just give it to me and you can go home and start your married life together. And don't expect your mother and father to come to your rescue, Cassandra. It was very easy to drop a little something in their drinks. They won't wake up in time to help, I'm afraid.'

Cass felt sick. She knew her ring would come to her rescue, but it only seemed to work if she was threatened personally. It wasn't going to get Noel out of trouble. She had no idea whether his emerald could help him. So far, it hadn't been put to the test.

Noel held up his hand. 'I would let

you have it if I could, Constantine. It doesn't have any special powers. Not that I've noticed, anyway. But there is one little problem — I can't get it off.'

Cass closed her eyes. That probably wasn't the most sensible thing to say, considering the circumstances.

Constantine frowned. 'Show me your hand.'

Now Cass could see what Noel was trying to do. The only way Constantine could get at the ring was to drop his shield, and then Noel could make a move. She geared herself up, ready to help out as soon as Constantine became vulnerable. He was tall, but slightly built, and she was sure Noel could easily overpower him.

Constantine moved closer but kept out of range. 'I've heard of charms becoming embedded once they've chosen their master, but in this case it is not a problem. Once the ring is detached from the host it will be easy to remove. I don't much care for bloodshed myself, but I know several club members who will quite enjoy performing an amputation.'

Noel looked around the cabin and shrugged dismissively. 'But your blood-thirsty club members aren't here right now, and you have no real powers, Lucien. We have magic. Together we can easily overpower you.'

Constantine mimicked Noel's shrug with one of his own. 'The thing is, Mr Police Detective, I don't need magic. I have a gun.' And the one Constantine had produced from his jacket pocket was pointing straight at Noel.

Cass moved closer and slipped her hand into Noel's, hoping it would look as if she was scared — which she was, of course; but she also wanted to know if he had a plan.

We can fire a bolt of electricity at him and hope it pierces his shield.

Yes, they could do that, but Constantine was holding a gun. Cass wondered if a bolt of lightning was faster than a bullet. She didn't really want to put it to the test. Noel gripped her hand even more tightly and when he raised his arm there was nothing she could do.

The electricity from their rings *was* faster. A streak of blue fire shot through Constantine's shield as if it wasn't there, spinning him round. Cass heard the gun hit the floor, but it was too late: Constantine had fired as he fell, the bullet hitting Noel high up in his chest. Before Cass could move, the door burst open and Dora ran in, closely followed by Hector.

Dora didn't waste time talking. She dropped to her knees beside Noel. He was sitting on the floor beside Constantine's inert body, looking slightly bewildered, and holding a hand to his chest.

'Get a towel from the bathroom, Cassie,' Dora said briskly. 'A clean one, if possible. I need to stop this bleeding.'

Cass ran into the tiny bathroom and grabbed a towel. She handed it to Dora, who ripped open Noel's shirt and found the wound. 'It's quite high up,' she said as she took the towel and folded it into a pad. 'Nowhere near his heart, thank goodness, but he's losing a lot of blood.'

Hector bent down beside her. 'It's an in-and-out,' he said. 'The bullet must still be around somewhere. Most of the blood is coming from the exit wound.'

He helped Dora roll Noel onto his side. Once they removed his shirt, Cass was shocked to see the amount of blood that had soaked into the pale carpet. 'I think I can cauterise it,' she said. 'Will that help?' When her parents both nodded, she dropped to her knees and pressed her hand against Noel's chest, hoping the sapphire in her ring was near the wound. There was an audible hiss and a slight smell of burnt flesh. When she took her hand away the hole in Noel's back had been replaced with a small circular burn scar. The bleeding had completely stopped.

'Do I need to do the same to the entry wound?' she asked.

Dora shook her head. 'You probably saved his life, Cassie, but he's going to have a nasty scar from that burn. He might prefer a few stiches at the front.'

Noel used his good arm to prop himself up. 'Keep her away from me, Dora. She's lethal with that ring.'

Cass managed to hug him without dislodging the towel. 'That's gratitude for you. Next time I'll leave you to bleed to death.'

Hector was bending down beside Constantine's still form. 'The lightning bolt that broke his shield stopped his heart, Cassandra. Do you want me to start it again?'

Now there's a question, she thought, but she nodded. She didn't want to be responsible for the death of anyone, even Constantine.

Hector pressed his fingers against Constantine's chest. 'I don't suppose you've got your handcuffs with you, Noel?'

Noel shook his head and winced. 'Damn, I shouldn't have done that. Tie him up with the cord from the bedside lamp. That always works in TV shows.'

'And I have scissors.' Dora produced a pair of nail scissors from her capacious handbag. 'We counteracted the drug Constantine gave us, but we suddenly noticed he'd disappeared. We thought he might have come to the cabins. Hector wanted to search for drugs while Lucien was out of the way, but luckily I persuaded him to come and find you both before he did anything else.'

While Hector secured Constantine's hands and feet with the lamp cord, Dora and Cass helped Noel shuffle to the sofa. Dora made a sling out of torn bedsheet and arranged Noel's arm in a more comfortable position. 'Hospital,' she said firmly. 'As soon as we get away from here.'

'Thank you, Dora.' Noel looked at Constantine, who still hadn't moved. 'Is he actually breathing? I need him alive to arrest him.'

Hector felt for a pulse. 'Yes, his heart rate is fine and he's breathing normally. But it might be a good idea to keep him unconscious for a bit.' He stopped speaking and tilted his head on one side. 'Did you hear that?'

Up until that moment, Cass's ears had been filled with the beating of her own heart. But now she could hear a faint sound, like the mewing of a kitten. It seemed to be coming from the back of the cabin.

A tiny kitchen opened off the living area and another door led to the bathroom. Hector picked up Constantine's gun and waked towards the only remaining door. Cass had assumed this was a bedroom, and when Hector flung open the door she was proved right. What she hadn't expected to see was a man trussed up like an oven-ready chicken. He had duct tape over his mouth, and more tape had been used to secure his arms and legs. His eyes were wide with fear when the door opened and he caught sight of Hector. Cass realised he must have heard the gunshot and thought his turn was coming next.

'Well, well, well,' Noel murmured from his seat on the sofa. 'Bradley Shelton. We wondered what Constantine had done with you.'

Hector gently removed the tape from Bradley's mouth. 'Constantine's out for the count, so you're safe now. How long have you been in here?'

Bradley rubbed his sore lips. 'He told me the police thought I'd murdered my mother and that they were looking for me. He said he'd let me stay here for a few days. Is my mother really dead?' Tears filled his eyes. 'We don't always get on, because she doesn't like me gambling, but I'd never hurt her.'

'Someone went to Mary's house looking for the emerald ring your father brought back from abroad,' Cass said. 'Your mother had to stay in hospital for a few days, but she's all right now.' She helped Hector cut Bradley free with Dora's nail scissors. 'You must have told someone about the ring.'

'Mr Constantine,' Bradley said guiltily. 'I was bragging about my gran

303

having a gold ring set with a big emerald. I thought he would let me run up a tab if he thought I could get my hands on something valuable. He asked a lot of questions about it, like whether it had an inscription on it. He seemed really interested.'

'I bet he did,' Hector muttered. 'He got one of the club members, a big man with the bat tattoo on his wrist, to visit your mother. He's the one who put her in hospital. We also know Constantine deals in drugs. We need to know where he hides his stuff, Bradley. Can you help us?'

'As far as I know it's mainly hash and pills,' Bradley said. 'Ketamine and stuff like that.' He paused. 'I know where he keeps all of it.'

Hector handed his gun to Noel. 'You two stay here and keep an eye on Constantine. If he wakes up and gives you any trouble, shoot him in the knee. That usually works. We'll take Bradley with us so he can show us where Constantine hides his drugs.'

Once Dora and Hector had gone, Cass sat down beside Noel. He looked so pale, she was afraid he'd pass out. 'I thought you were going to die,' she said.

Noel managed something like a laugh. 'So did I, for a minute or two. When I felt that bullet thud against my chest, I thought my time was up.' He turned his head to look at her. 'Thank you for stopping the bleeding so quickly. You probably saved my life.'

'Then we're quits. You saved my life once and now I've saved yours, so I don't have to be your slave anymore.'

'Don't you believe it, darling. Once you put that heart on your finger, you'll belong to me — every beautiful, sexy inch of you.' When she moved her head from his shoulder and sat up, he stopped her speaking by pressing his finger against her lips. 'I'm too weak to argue. I might have a relapse any minute and need the kiss of life.'

Cass decided prevention was better than cure, but before she could do anything Constantine began to stir. His eyelids flickered, but his eyes remained shut. After a few minutes he appeared to lose consciousness again.

Noel pointed the gun at him. 'If he moves again, Cass, I'm going to shoot him, so this might be a good time to call for reinforcements. Can you hand me my phone?'

Cass passed the phone to Noel, but her eyes stayed on Constantine. What if his shield was still strong enough to keep out a bullet? Then what would they do? Perhaps magic really was more powerful than the technology of the real world. She looked down at her sapphire, confident it could keep her safe, and wondered when her perspective had changed so drastically. Maybe a close look at death had made her see things differently. Magic was now part of her life — a life that included Noel Raven; and for that she would always be eternally grateful.

It wasn't so much an engagement party as a family-and-friends get-together. Noel invited his grandmother, because she was dying to meet Dora, and Liz popped in for a cup of tea. Spring had arrived, and the French doors were open onto the patio.

Cass and Noel had worked out a setting for the ruby heart, and it now sat in glorious isolation on her left hand. She didn't wear much jewellery as a rule, and with a ring on each hand and the sapphire earrings glittering in her ears, she felt enough was enough. Noel had given Mary a good price for the emerald ring — much more than it was worth, Cass told him — but to Noel the ring was priceless. With it on his finger, he was a prince; without it, he was a police detective.

Hector handed Cass a glass of champagne and sat down beside her. 'I have a friend who is a professor of ancient languages, and I asked him if he could decipher the markings on your ring. I had a feeling they might be letters from an archaic language, and I was right. I had the translation before I gave you the ring for your birthday, but it wasn't until you showed me the hieroglyphics on the back of Noel's ring that I realised their significance.' When Cass just looked at him in silence, he smiled. 'There is one word on each ring; and the word on your sapphire ring, when translated, is 'together'.'

Cass was quiet for a moment, letting her thoughts settle. Now everything made sense. 'You don't have to tell me the word on Noel's emerald ring,' she said. 'I already know. It's 'invincible'.'

Hector took her hand in his. 'I may not show it, Cassandra, but I care about you. I knew you would eventually meet someone you wanted to marry, but I couldn't let you give yourself to just anyone. The man you marry must be very special.'

Cass looked across the sunlit court-yard to where her future husband was sitting with his grandmother. He saw her looking at him and smiled, raising his glass in a salute.

'He is,' she said.

We do hope that you have enjoyed reading this large print book.

Did you know that all of our titles are available for purchase?

We publish a wide range of high quality large print books including:
Romances, Mysteries, Classics General Fiction Non Fiction and Westerns

Special interest titles available in large print are:
The Little Oxford Dictionary Music Book, Song Book Hymn Book, Service Book

Also available from us courtesy of Oxford University Press:
Young Readers' Dictionary (large print edition) Young Readers' Thesaurus (large print edition)

For further information or a free brochure, please contact us at:
Ulverscroft Large Print Books Ltd., The Green, Bradgate Road, Anstey, Leicester, LE7 7FU, England.
Tel: (00 44) 0116 236 4325
Fax: (00 44) 0116 234 0205

A MOMENT LIKE THIS

Rena George

When Jenna Maitland's cousin Joss flees the responsibilities of their family's department store empire in Yorkshire, he escapes to Cornwall to follow his true calling and paint. Accompanied by the mysterious Gil Ryder, Jenna sets off south to find him. Once in Cornwall, Jenna finds herself becoming increasingly attracted to Gil — but is warned off by the attractive Victoria Symington, who appears to regard Gil as her own. Meanwhile, Joss's whereabouts has been discovered — but he is refusing to return . . .

BROKEN PROMISES

Chrissie Loveday

The greatest day of Carolyn's life has arrived: she is to marry her beloved Henry. But when she gets to the church, it becomes clear that something is terribly wrong. The groom has disappeared! Devastated, Carolyn is supported by her brother and his girlfriend as she tries to pick up the pieces of her life. When she meets kind, caring Jed, she feels as if she really is over Henry — but is this just a rebound? And will she ever find out why she was jilted at the altar?